REVEREND MARGOT QUADE

COZY MYSTERIES BOOKS 1-3

S.E. BIGLOW

INTO THE LION'S DEN

Into the Lion's Den

S.E. BIGLOW

For information contact; www.sarah-biglow.com

Copyedited by: Liza Street

Proofreading and Formatting by: Under Wraps Publishing Services

Cover Design by: Deranged Doctor Design

Published by Carter and Bradley Publishing in Secrets and Suspense: August 2019

Published by Sarah Biglow: March 2020

10 9 8 7 6 5 4 3 2 1

Homecoming was bittersweet. After fourteen months serving her country, Margot Quade set foot back in the small town of Port Marie, Vermont in the dead of winter. At present, she sat in the front seat of her car—a beat-up Honda—staring at the imposing structure that was the Nesbit home. With a large circular driveway and a columned front porch, it screamed wealth. Margot was never much for such obvious signs of money; but she'd accepted the dinner invitation from Derek

Nesbit as a chance to catch up with a former brother-in-arms.

The heater blasted stale air into Margot's face, making the strands of her blond bob flutter under her nose and into her mouth. Time to brave the elements and the gaudy exterior, meet her friend's relatives. It was just dinner. Snow fell outside her window in thick flakes as she donned a hat. After climbing out of the car, she raced up the driveway, careful of her footing. It wouldn't make a very good first impression if she fell before even making it to the door. Ducking under the relative safety of the porch roof, she knocked on the front door.

No response.

Shivering in the bitter cold, she tugged off her glove and dug around in her coat pocket for her phone. *Maybe I got the date or time wrong?* The excessive heat of the Middle East threw off her New Englander sensibilities. Her exposed fingers turned red in a matter of seconds. She flipped to her calendar and found that she had not gotten the date or time wrong. Something seemed off.

She knocked again. She was about to peer through one of the fogged over front windows when the door squeaked on its hinges and opened inward. An older Latina woman with graying temples studied Margot in silence.

Margot tucked her ungloved hand under her arm to keep it warm as the woman continued to eye her. "Hi, I'm Margot. Derek invited me for dinner."

The woman smiled, but it didn't reach her eyes. They remained pinched at the corners with worry. "Please come in," she responded in lightly accented English.

Margot darted into the large front hall, grateful for the heat. She shed her coat, hat and remaining glove. The woman dutifully took them, hanging them on a coat rack next to an old-school radiator.

"Everyone is in the dining room," the woman said and gestured for Margot to follow her.

Margot stopped in front of the large staircase that dominated the rest of entryway. At the end of each balustrades sat a lifelike full-sized lion and lioness. She stepped closer and shivered—not from the cold, but from the dead look in the animals' eyes. She suspected they had once been alive. As she left the animals to guard their posts, she doubted she would get along with Derek's aunt and uncle.

"Warren, that's unnecessary," a female voice said from a distance.

"Just drop it!" Derek's voice echoed from deeper in the house.

The volume of his voice drew Margot with faster steps through an industrial kitchen to the large dining room. The table could easily seat twenty, perhaps thirty people. Only five places were set at the far end.

Four of the chairs were presently occupied. Derek was on his feet leaning over a man with snowy white hair. The woman beside him bore a striking resemblance to the older woman who'd invited Margot into the house with cinnamon-colored skin and jet-black hair pulled into a loose braid draped over one shoulder.

"I hope I'm not interrupting," Margot said, making her presence known.

Movement in the room stopped and Derek turned at the sound of her voice. Their eyes met and she noticed the fat lip and the bruise under his right eye. Despite his injuries, he stood at attention, hands behind his back. Even though his family was wealthy, Derek had exhibited none of the airs she'd expected. He was polite and kind, ready to help a fellow soldier no matter the task. He was often the first awake in the morning for cleaning duties, even when it wasn't his assignment. Perhaps that was why they had hit it off so well. "Ma'am," he said out of training and habit.

Margot tried to give a kind smile. She understood that the formalities drilled into them in the army were hard to break and even as a Chaplain, she'd outranked him. "It's just Margot these days."

Derek took longer to relax from his position than Margot thought was really necessary. The young woman at his side got to her feet and offered Margot her hand. "I'm Catalina, Derek's wife, and that's my mother, Rosalinda."

Derek hadn't stopped talking about his fiancée, Cat, while he and Margot had been completing their deployment. He'd been so excited to marry her. She hadn't made the connection, though, that Catalina was the daughter of his family's housekeeper.

"It's nice to meet you. Derek talked about you all the time."

Catalina smiled and let out a soft giggle. "Only good things I hope."

"Always. I'm sorry I missed the big day," Margot replied.

Neither Derek nor Catalina responded to her statement. Mrs. Nesbit stood and rounded the end of the dining table to greet Margot.

"Leave it to my nephew to not introduce us to his guest. I'm Mary Ellen Nesbit and this is my husband Warren. You can call me Mary."

Warren Nesbit, upon closer inspection, was far heavier set than Margot would have imagined. From the stories she'd heard as a child, he'd always been an imposing man in great health. He looked more like an ordinary man in his sixties, having fallen victim to the ravages of time and aging.

"Margot Quade."

Mary arched a brow in her nephew's direction. "So, this is the Reverend you've been talking about for months at church?"

Margot blushed. "He really shouldn't have." Serving as a Chaplain had given her a purpose—one fostered from growing up in the church. That same church now sat leaderless after her mentor, Reverend Patrick Hawley, retired over a year earlier. Coming home, she wasn't sure where she fit.

"There's no one better for the position and you know it," Derek argued.

Derek believed Margot was perfect to take over leading the Christian portion of the new interfaith church, a sentiment Reverend Hawley shared. Margot didn't object to leading a congregation, if it turned out to be God's path for her.

"Derek mentioned you helped to keep up morale overseas," Mary said.

Margot couldn't deny she and Derek had bonded during their time abroad. She regretted that the difference in their upbringing—Mary and Warren raised Derek on the wealthier side of town—meant they'd only connected as adults.

"Enough of this religious talk. It's time to eat," Warren barked, not moving from his chair.

Rosalinda, eyes cast downward, disappeared into the kitchen and carried out plates of roasted winter squash and carrots. Next came perfectly formed dinner rolls and a platter of white fish. Last, she brought out a bottle of red wine, setting it by Warren's place.

"Aren't you joining us?" Margot asked as Rosalinda beat a hasty exit out of the room.

"The help doesn't eat with us," Warren answered abruptly as he struggled to free the cork from the wine bottle.

Margot bristled at his words. She couldn't fathom how Derek had grown up under this man's guidance and turned out so differently. She sat beside Catalina and leaned close. She whispered, "Is he always like this?"

"Since Derek came back."

Decorum dictated that Margot accept the food offered by her hosts, but she barely ate anything, the tension in the room too uncomfortable for her liking. Something was wrong in this house.

"So, did you see combat like Derek?" Mary asked as Rosalinda carried out a carafe of coffee.

"Aunt Mary, you can't ask things like that," Derek said quickly.

"Well, you haven't told us much about what she actually did. Or what you did, for that matter."

"Careful, Mary. You'll trigger his post-traumatic stress." Warren snickered.

Derek's fists tightened around the coffee cup in front of him. Margot had seen the tell-tale signs before, and not just in her fellow soldiers. She'd woken up in cold sweats in the middle of the night since her return home, swearing she'd heard a noise that could have been a bomb. She understood why Derek had been slim on the details of his service. There were some things one didn't share with civilians and others that civilians couldn't understand without being there in the moment.

"I didn't see much combat, no. But I saw the aftermath," Margot said in a measured tone. Just enough to give a response, but not enough to divulge their shared history.

"Well, Derek mentioned you saved his life. Thank you. Thank you for getting my husband back to me safely," Catalina said with a sincere look.

"It wasn't just me, but you're welcome."

Without warning or ceremony, Warren stood, unsteady on his feet, and teetered out of the room. The moment he was out of earshot and sight, the remaining Nesbits relaxed. Mary disappeared into the kitchen, returning with Rosalinda behind her carrying a dinner plate. She sat beside her daughter and ate in silence.

"I'm very sorry you had to see my husband like that," she said to Margot.

"He's turned into such a prick," Derek said.

"He didn't used to be like this," Mary said, as if her nephew hadn't spoken. "I think Derek going away overseas took a toll on him."

He wouldn't be the first family member to exhibit strain from a soldier's absence. I know that feeling. "War can be difficult on families. Did he ever serve?"

"Uncle Warren?" Derek scoffed and rolled his eyes. "Yeah right. He never worked a day in his life. I know I didn't act like it, but our family money goes back a long way. Everything you see here, he inherited."

Derek stood up, breathing heavily, before

storming out of the room. Margot watched him go in shock.

Catalina gave Margot a brief apologetic look and then followed her husband. They left Margot alone with Rosalinda and Mary. Mary studied the contents of her coffee cup in silence, refusing to acknowledge Derek's tirade. Their attitudes and behavior made Margot wonder whether they had actually been to church of late. Perhaps they needed to be around people who shared their beliefs.

"He wasn't happy about their wedding," Rosalinda muttered so softly Margot almost missed it all together.

"Why not?" Margot asked.

Mary spoke up. "Warren thought they should have a traditional church wedding. It's what we had, and since we had no children of our own, he never had the opportunity to host it. He felt cheated."

"They went to the Town Hall, just the two of them. No minister, witnesses or anything,"

Rosalinda explained, her voice growing stronger.

"Warren was furious," Mary added.

The tension within the ranks made sense. From the little interaction she'd had with Warren, Margot could pin him as the type of man who wouldn't easily give up control of situations and people in his orbit. Having his nephew—someone he viewed like a son—marry in a manner he didn't approve of would make him upset.

"That's not the only reason he is angry," Rosalinda added, her voice softening again.

"Why else would he be upset?" Margot probed.

"He isn't happy that Derek married the daughter of the help."

Margot believed Rosalinda's statement, given Warren's reference to "the help." Perhaps this was a test to see if she could counsel this family through this troubling time. Maybe this was God's way of showing her she had a purpose in Port Marie. If Derek believed in her abilities enough to convince the congregation to call her their new minister, the least she could do was prove them right by helping him and his family in a time of stress. First, she wanted to talk to Warren and see if there was any truth to what everyone else had shared with her.

"Would you excuse me for a moment?" Margot stood before anyone gave her permission and made her way out of the dining room in the direction Warren had disappeared. She found him sitting in a large wing-backed leather chair in front of a roaring fire.

"Mr. Nesbit? Or would you rather, Warren? It's Margot. I was hoping we could speak for a few minutes?"

Silence.

She stepped around the side of his chair and something sticky caught at the bottom of her boot. She looked down to see an empty scotch glass lying on the hardwood floor. How had none of them heard it fall? And why wasn't Warren moving to pick it up? Instead, he sat unmoving and unseeing in the chair. With a sinking feeling, Margot pressed her fingers to the man's throat. No pulse.

Warren Nesbit was dead.

2

Margot had some experience administering last rites to those who wouldn't make it home from the battlefield, but she had never happened upon a dead body before. Footsteps drew Margot's attention away from the man and she looked up to see Derek standing in the room's doorway.

"He's dead," she announced, the words sounding strange to her ears.

"That's not funny."

She shook her head. "I'm not kidding."

Derek stalked over to the chair and bent down to study his uncle. "He was fine twenty minutes ago."

"He's not now. We should call the police."

Derek's eyes narrowed. "Why the police?"

"They'd be the ones who can call a medical examiner. And, if he was fine only half an hour ago, it's unlikely he died of natural causes. They'll want to investigate."

Derek didn't look pleased by Margot's statement, but he pulled his cell phone from his pocket and dialed 9-1-1. He stepped back away from his uncle's body, still close enough for Margot to hear the dispatcher on the other end of the line.

"9-1-1, what is your emergency?"

"This is Derek Nesbit. My uncle Warren is dead. You need to send someone please."

Margot didn't pay attention as Derek verified the street address. She bent over to study Warren's body in closer detail, careful not to touch anything else with her bare hands. There were odd flecks around his mouth, but they didn't mean anything to her. *He wasn't this sweaty earlier, was he?* Even with a fire burning in the hearth, his body shouldn't have taken on such a sheen. She also noted tiny pinpricks on his left index finger and there was also a tiny hole in the thigh of his left pantleg. Up close, she spotted the raw skin on his knuckles from where he'd punched something. *Or someone.* Derek's injuries made sense now.

"I ... I need to tell Aunt Mary," Derek said, pulling Margot from her investigation.

"Yes, that's a good idea. Derek, I'm so sorry for your loss." Margot reached out a hand to give her friend support, but he shied away.

He left the room without a word. His heavy footfalls thudded on the wooden floor leading into the dining room. Margot retreated there as well and found it empty. She heard the clatter of dishes and the sound of running water in the kitchen, so she followed the cacophony to find Catalina and Rosalinda standing side by side at the sink doing dishes. Before she could speak, a loud knock on the front door drew her attention.

Most likely the police. There were benefits to living in a small town: rapid law enforcement response among them.

"Who is that?" Catalina wondered aloud.

Margot knew they needed to hear the news, but not from her. No matter how many stories Derek told them about her, she was still a stranger. So, she darted back into the front hall, ignoring the imposing silhouettes of the lion and lioness on the balustrades and pulled the heavy door open.

Snow swirled outside, the storm having picked up since her arrival. There was little chance she could get her car out of this mess until the storm stopped raging.

"Sam?" she said, surprised by the person standing on the other side of the threshold.

Samantha Raymond had been only a year behind Margot in school. She also happened to be Margot's first cousin.

"What are you doing here?" Sam questioned, her gaze narrowing. They hadn't spoken since Margot's return from active duty.

"The family invited me for dinner," she answered.

Realizing it was rude to keep her cousin standing in the cold, Margot stepped back and allowed Sam to enter the warmth of the house. Sam stomped the snow from her boots and looked around.

"I didn't know you even knew the Nesbits," Sam commented.

"Derek and I served together."

"Oh."

Just as Margot gestured for Sam to follow her into the kitchen, a high-pitched wail echoed from deep within the house. Four sets of footsteps thundered toward the sound, converging in the sitting room to find Mary draped over Warren's body, Derek standing off to one side. It seemed the gravity of the situation was finally settling over Derek. But was responding in true military fashion, he'd been trained to hide his feelings at the loss of one of his own. He squared his shoulders and a hardness had taken over his facial features. Anyone who didn't know what he was doing would assume he had something to hide.

"Oh my God," Catalina rasped at the sight of Warren's prone form in the chair. She raced to her husband's side and buried her face in his shoulder. He barely moved.

"Mrs. Nesbit, you need to let go now," Sam said, her voice soft.

Mary blinked through thick tears, confusion on her face. "I don't understand. Why are you here?"

"I called the police, Aunt Mary," Derek answered, his tone robotic.

"But, why?" Mary repeated.

Sam let out a sigh. "By your reaction, I take it this was a shock."

Mary wiped tears away from her cheeks with the back of her hand. "Of course, it's a shock. My husband wouldn't just drop dead."

Sam nodded. "Which is why I'm here. I need to investigate what happened." She turned to look at Margot. "Let's start with your statement and give the family some time to collect themselves."

3

<hr>

Margot followed Sam back to the kitchen, where the sink's faucet was still running. Feeling uneasy, Margot busied herself with shutting it off and stacking plates into the dishwasher.

"How do you know the Nesbits?" Sam asked.

"As I said before, Derek and I served together. We became friends and when I came home, we reconnected. He invited me to have dinner with his family." Margot faced her cousin. They had been good friends growing up and had remained so even after Margot followed God's calling and attended seminary. Sam had never been a spiritual person, but she'd believed in doing good and helping those who couldn't help themselves. Margot had thought Sam understood why she'd joined the military—to follow the path the Lord had set for her. While Margot was overseas Sam had refused to email her back and wouldn't accept her calls.

"I'm sorry," Margot said, filling the awkward silence between them.

"For what?"

"For whatever I did to make you so upset with me."

Sam heaved a sigh. "I'm not mad at you. I'm mad at myself."

Margot moved to lean against the counter beside her cousin. "What do you have to be mad about?"

"You made something of yourself. You

ran into danger and all I did was sit home in Port Marie."

"Sam, come on. You put on a badge every day. At any time, you could walk right into danger's path."

Sam snorted. "Let's be real, nothing that dangerous ever happens in Port Marie."

Margot gestured toward the dining room. "Well, at least you've got a mystery to solve. I might as well give you my statement."

Sam nodded as she pulled out a notepad and pen. "Okay, tell me what you saw."

Margot fingered the cross and dog tags at her throat. She'd worn them this way since she arrived in the Middle East. It comforted her. It also helped to center her thoughts. "I came for dinner, like I said. When I arrived, there was some argument going on."

"Could you tell about what?"

"No. But Derek and Warren were going at it. Derek had a bloody lip and a bruise under his eye. They looked fresh. I noticed some abrasions on Warren's knuckles when I found him."

"So, you were the first person to notice he'd died?"

"Yes. He said some rather insensitive things during dinner. I don't think he's pleased with the fact that Derek and Catalina got married. Or the way they went about it. He stormed out of dinner. I wanted to talk to him, to see if I could try and help smooth things over. That's when I went looking for him. I found him in the other room. It must of happened quickly."

"What sort of things did he say during dinner?" Sam probed.

Margot hesitated. It wasn't her place to share Warren's diatribe. And she felt bad enough already with what she'd said. She'd been taught not to speak ill of the dead. "He referred to Rosalinda, Catalina's mother, as 'the help.' Catalina's mother mentioned he also seemed unhappy that Catalina and Derek went to Town Hall to get married."

Sam scribbled notes on her pad and wet her lips. "I'd tell you not to leave town in case I have more questions, but you won't be able to get out of here anyway. The storm is only supposed to get progressively worse through the night."

"I'm guessing I can't hitch a ride with you?"

"Sorry, I wouldn't want to be accused of giving you preferential treatment just because we're family."

She would be stuck in the Nesbit home for the foreseeable future with a potential killer.

"If you'll excuse me, I need to see about getting a forensic team here. It could be difficult with the storm. Also, please let Derek know I need to talk to him next."

Margot headed to the dining room when she stopped. "I know you think his reaction means he did something to his uncle, but he's doing what the military trained him to do ... To compartmentalize his emotions. Just remember that, okay?"

"Just tell him."

Margot made the trek back to the library in what was becoming a familiar route. The women had left and Derek stood in front of the fireplace. The flames had died down to embers.

"What are they going to do with his body?" Derek asked.

"Officer Raymond is calling in a forensic team to look at and move the body. But with the storm, it may take some time. She wants to talk to you next," Margot relayed.

"You should stay."

"I'm here for whatever you need, Derek. You know that."

He shook his head. "I meant for the night. It's not safe to drive in this mess."

"I appreciate the hospitality. Now, please go give her your statement."

He took a few steps past his uncle's body and stopped. "It looks bad, doesn't it? That we fought."

He wasn't wrong. Margot had sensed something amiss when she arrived. Still *Derek's not the type of person to commit murder.* She'd seen him run into danger to save his fellow man. She couldn't believe he was capable of such an unthinkable act. He didn't need her suspicion right now. She placed a hand on his shoulder. He didn't shy away this time. "I know the truth will come out. Just be honest with her."

Other questions swirled in the back of her mind. *How long had Warren felt that way about Rosalinda and her daughter? How long had she been working for the Nesbits?* Most people in town, even those with money, didn't have live-in housekeepers anymore.

The unanswered questions nagged at

Margot. She wasn't one to stick her nose where it didn't belong, but this whole situation unsettled her. She had every confidence in Sam's investigative abilities, but surely her cousin wouldn't mind some extra help.

First, Margot needed to make sure her staying the night was okay with Mary. She wandered the first floor, glimpsing Sam and Derek in the kitchen before she made her way up the winding staircase to the second floor. She turned right and walked down the hall. The doors proved to be concealing extra guest bedrooms and a bathroom. The last door on the left was a linen closet. She turned back to check the other end of the floor when Mary appeared. She'd stopped crying, but her skin was pale and her eyes were red-rimmed. Her eyes widened in surprise upon seeing Margot.

"I'm sorry, Mrs. Nesbit. I didn't mean to startle you," Margot apologized, reverting to the formality a guest should show a host.

Mary blinked a time or two before putting on a small smile. "I was just … is the police officer still here?"

"Yes. She's called for help with Warren's remains. She needs to speak with you. Rosalinda and Catalina, too. Just to take your statements."

"But we don't know anything."

"She's trying to piece together his last few hours. Having as many perspectives as possible is useful. And I want you to know, I'm here to help. Grief can be confusing and unpredictable. If you need help with his service, I'll do what I can. I know I'm not actually the minister, but I'm sure the board of Deacons wouldn't mind me coordinating on your behalf."

"That's kind of you. I'll think about it." She glanced out one of the nearby windows. "It's picking up out there. You shouldn't drive in this."

"Derek already offered to let me stay the night. I hope that's not too intrusive."

"Of course not. Come on, I'll make up a guest room for you."

Margot caught sight of flashing lights through the thick, swirling storm. Perhaps they would get some answers sooner rather than later.

"Mary, can I ask you something?" She met the older woman at the linen closet.

"About what?"

"I had a question about Warren's health of late?"

"His health?"

"Had he been feeling all right?"

"He was fine. I mean, he was diagnosed with diabetes last year, but he was managing it."

"With insulin injections," Margot muttered.

"How'd you know?"

"It's a common treatment." It also explained the pin prick on his finger and the hole in his pants. He'd been checking his blood sugar and administering insulin shots.

"Right. Forgive me. I'm … distracted."

"I understand."

"Aunt Mary." Derek's voice boomed up from the bottom of the staircase, echoing oddly in the upstairs acoustics.

"I suppose it's my turn, then," Mary murmured.

Margot took the sheets and fresh towels from Mary's outstretched hands. "I can handle this. Thank you."

"The room just there will be fine. It's next to Derek's." Mary waved a hand at one of the partially closed doors as she made her way down the stairs and out of view.

Mary's comment struck Margot as strange. If Derek and Catalina had been married for a few months now, wouldn't they share a bedroom? When she stuck her head into the room Mary had denoted as her nephew's, no items of women's clothing or other feminine touches marked the space. Margot filed that away as another oddity in what was shaping up to be a perplexing mystery.

4

____

Margot took her time making up the guest bed. She wanted to consider the information she had so far and stay out of Sam's way. It wouldn't do to have her cousin angry with her after they'd finally reconnected. Who would have thought they would begin to repair their relationship over a dead body? Margot settled on the end of the bed, closed her eyes, and bowed her head.

For her, prayer had never been about the words she said. She needed to be in a quiet place, at peace. Margot focused on her breathing, how each inhale and exhale felt in her chest. It had given her solace during the late nights and early mornings overseas.

She had faith that whatever had befallen Warren Nesbit would be solved. She believed in her cousin's abilities and in the notion that good always triumphs evil. If someone in this house knew something—which was likely given that they had been living together for so long—they would bring it to Sam's attention. Still, questions swirled in Margot's mind. *Where had Derek gone after he'd stormed out?* Mary's behavior was strange, too. People grieved differently, but her reluctance to answer questions about Warren was suspicious. And Margot hadn't spoken with Rosalinda or Catalina in depth, but she suspected neither of them held high opinions of Warren given his comments at dinner. Their reactions, or lack thereof, told

Margot they were not new sentiments and they'd heard those words—or worse—spoken before.

"There you are." Sam's voice pulled Margot from her contemplation.

"What's going on?"

"I had some follow up questions. I need you to come back downstairs."

Margot pushed herself off the bed and followed without a word. They traipsed back down the spiral stairs and Sam led her into the sitting room where technicians were busy tending to the scene and Warren's body. Aside from the forensics team, the room appeared the same as it had when Margot first happened upon Warren.

"What do you need to know?" Margot looked Sam in the eye.

"First, the techs said they found a fingerprint on his neck. Did you or anyone else touch the body?"

Margot's heart sank. She'd been foolish.

"I did … to check for a pulse. I can give you prints to exclude me if that would help."

"Probably for the best. Did you notice anything else unusual when you found him?"

"Unusual how?'

"Just anything that seemed off about his body."

Margot tried to recall what she'd noted when she was doing a cursory examination of the dead man. "I mean, I noticed the pinhole pricks in his pants and his index finger. But that's from testing his blood sugar and insulin injections for diabetes. At least that's what Mary told me."

Sam's brow furrowed. "She mentioned nothing about diabetes."

"She's still in shock," Margot said, though she didn't really believe her own words.

"What about the fire? Was it hot in here?"

"I guess so. The fire was going."

"Were there any other fires going in the house?"

"Not that I noticed. In all honesty, until I came in here, I'd only been in the foyer, the kitchen, and the dining room."

"We will run some tests but I can't shake the feeling something happened here. I don't think he keeled over of natural causes."

Margot wanted to agree with Sam's assessment, but she wasn't ready to believe any of the family capable of such an act. "I'm sure you'll figure it out."

"We'll be taking his body when they're done."

"I'm staying the night." Margot didn't add that she'd keep an eye on everyone, but the understanding seemed to pass between the two women.

Sam took one last look around the room and stowed her notepad. "I need to talk to everyone together. I think everyone is in the dining room."

Margot traced the now-familiar path back to the ornate dining room. As Sam had said, the four remaining occupants sat around the table looking glum. Derek poured a mostly empty bottle of whiskey into a glass, then tossed the contents back in one gulp.

"We're taking the body now," Sam said. "Until we determine a cause of death, none of you should leave town. I may have follow-up questions."

"Yes, of course," Catalina answered for the group.

Despite the house not being hers, Margot escorted her cousin back to the foyer. Wind howled outside as they opened the front door. "I'm sorry I didn't write you or call while you were away," Sam whispered.

"We've got all the time in the world to make up for it now," Margot replied and pulled her cousin into a quick, one-armed hug.

Sam donned her jacket and started out through the thigh-high drifts to her car. In short order, the forensics team trotted toward their van carrying Warren's body, shrouded in a body bag. Margot shoved the door closed behind them, exhaustion from the evening's events hitting her. From the kitchen, she heard Derek's voice rising in pitch.

"I can damn well drink if I want. I'm a grown man."

He staggered into the foyer, refusing to meet Margot's gaze. He pulled himself up the stairs by the railing, Catalina hot on his heels. Rosalinda and Mary followed soon after, leaving Margot to bring up the rear. She shed her pants and blouse, leaving her in a long-sleeved undershirt before crawling beneath the blankets. She hoped sleep would carry her away and the whole tragic affair would make more sense in the light of day.

5

Cries woke Margot from a dead sleep. She sat straight up in bed, disoriented by the unfamiliar and darkened surroundings. She looked left and right before memories of the evening came back to her.

The cries grew louder and she couldn't ignore them any longer. She fumbled for her pants, tugging them on in haste. In the pitch-black darkness of the room, she was back in the Middle East. Her breathing grew short and ragged as she eased open the bedroom door. She bent low, pressing her body to the wall, her ears straining to pick up on the cries. She closed her eyes to allow her ears to be the stronger sense. The cries leapt out from her left. Coming from the next bedroom.

Derek's.

She crept along the wall, easing the door open. There was just as little light in the room as had been in her own. She fumbled for a light switch, but thought better. She didn't need to blind them both. Instead she waited, allowing her eyes to adjust to the dark. Finally, she could make out Derek's thrashing form in the bed. His arms flailed above his head. She moved along the plush carpeting to stand beside the bed. This close, she could make out the sheen of sweat on his brow.

"No, get down!" he moaned, his entire body tossing from side to side. "Abrams, wait!"

Breath caught in Margot's throat. She knew the nightmare that had trapped him. During their tour of duty, rebels ambushed their convoy and one of their fellow soldiers, Peter Abrams, had taken the brunt of the shrapnel. He hadn't made it home. Margot and Derek had stayed with him, holding tight to his hands as he passed away.

"Soldier, wake up," Margot hissed, hoping her authoritative tone would draw him from the memory.

Derek continued to whimper and toss and turn. Margot needed to take a more drastic action. She seized him by both shoulders and shook him. "Private Nesbit, wake up."

He shot up, eyes wide and unfocused. His body tensed until he blinked, coming back to reality. Hair stuck to his forehead and his hands shook as he turned to look at Margot. Confusion turned to shame.

"It will be all right," she whispered, giving his shoulders a firm squeeze.

He didn't speak until Margot turned on the lights, bathing them in a pale-yellow glow. His skin was pale, almost ashen, and the bruise under his eye stood out even more. The split in his lip looked angry and raw.

"You shouldn't have to see me like this," he whispered, his voice hoarse.

"Don't be ridiculous. You're going through a very difficult time. It's bound to bring up bad memories."

"It should have been me driving." He stared down at his hands as they continued to shake.

"You can't blame yourself for surviving. There is always a plan, even if we can't see it at the time. You had to survive to come home and marry the love of your life."

"We haven't been able to share a room since I got back," he admitted.

That explained the lack of a feminine touch in the room. She wanted to comfort him, to tell him that it would all get better, but she didn't want to mislead him. She wasn't a counselor, not in that sense. She couldn't give him the psychological help he needed. She doubted he had even sought treatment.

"Have you told her why?" Margot asked.

He shook his head. "She wouldn't understand."

"Because she wasn't there. She didn't see how scared Peter was when he realized he wouldn't make it."

"I still see the look in his eyes when he stopped breathing."

Margot understood. Some nights, she too couldn't shake the image of their friend dying in their arms. "I think Catalina has more strength than you give her credit for. She married you, knowing you had seen combat. She's your support system now. You need to lean on her, to trust her."

"I know and I want to, but I'm scared. I haven't told anyone."

Including his uncle. Who'd seemed so dismissive of his possible PTSD diagnosis. "Is that why you were fighting with your uncle earlier? Because he didn't understand what you've been through and what you've lost?"

"No. I don't know what happened while we were deployed but he was a different man when I came home. So angry and mean. You heard the things he said about Cat's mother. He never used to be like that. He was always kind. She was a Guatemalan immigrant. She was pregnant when they hired her. They let her live with us and I grew up with Cat. I think that's why we fell in love. I couldn't imagine my life without her. But they paid Rosalinda more than most folks make in entry-level jobs. I mean, she wasn't making six figures or anything, but she could have moved out ages ago and gotten a decent place of her own. She stayed because we are her family. Until Uncle Warren started to treat her like she wasn't a person."

Margot let Derek's words sink in. The man Derek described as having raised him and taken in a woman who needed a job and a place to raise her child didn't jive with the one she'd met last night. It raised more questions about what had happened with him in Derek's absence.

"Was he diagnosed with diabetes before you deployed?"

"No. That happened after I left. As far as I knew, it was manageable and he was doing fine. I don't get why he became so angry and hateful toward everyone."

"It is a mystery," she agreed. One she committed to solving. She wouldn't be stepping on Sam's toes if she was simply trying to determine why a man who had been such a pillar of the community had turned into such a despicable person.

"I'm okay now," Derek said, wiping sweat from his face with the hem of his night shirt.

"Are you sure? Why don't I get you a glass of water?"

After a moment of contemplation, Derek nodded. "Thanks."

Margot padded down the hall to the staircase, shivering at the imposing shadows of the lions as she passed. In the early morning darkness, they seemed poised to stalk her like prey, ready to pounce. Taking a deep breath, she made her way to the first floor, leaving the beasts behind. She was about to enter the kitchen when a clang caught her off guard. She stopped, listening to see if the sound repeated. When it didn't, she continued into the kitchen and searched for a light. She found the switch on the wall and flooded the space with fluorescent light. Rosalinda stood in the center of the kitchen, a startled expression on her face.

"I'm sorry, I didn't mean to surprise you. I was just getting a glass of water," Margot said.

Rosalinda paused, her hands clutched to her chest for a moment before she relaxed. "I am sorry, too. With everything that's happened, I can't sleep. So sometimes I like to clean."

Margot nodded and stood immobile. "Could you point me to the water glasses?"

Rosalinda let out a small hiccup of nervous laughter and pointed to the cabinet to Margot's left. "On the bottom shelf."

Margot busied herself with filling the cup. Rosalinda disappeared past her and back upstairs. Margot took her time heading back up. Derek's nightmare about Peter's death dredged up her own memories of that particular loss. If she closed her eyes, she could still feel the sand digging into her palms as Peter clutched her hand, his blood making their fingers slick. Derek needed a brave face now and she pushed the memory down. She kept her head down as she darted up the stairs. The tiny hairs on the nape of her neck bristled and she turned to find the hallway empty. Despite the fact she was alone, her body refused to ignore the warning that she was being watched.

"Get a grip," she chided herself and returned to Derek's room to find him still sitting in bed. Thankfully, he looked a little less frazzled. She pushed the glass into his waiting hands. "Here. This should help."

Margot stood over him and watched as he drank the contents, ever the motherly figure. He set the empty glass on the nightstand and settled back beneath the blankets.

"You don't have to stay and watch me sleep," he said with a half-smile.

"Sorry. Habits are hard to break," she answered and left him to go back to her room.

She was surprised the commotion hadn't woken the rest of the house. Still, she couldn't shake the feeling of someone watching her. She glanced over her shoulder one last time before she returned to the guest room and shut the door.

6

Sunlight filtered through the gauzy blinds, falling across Margot's eyes. She moaned, throwing a hand over her face to block the light. Sounds of movement came from the hall. She sat up, smoothing what felt like bedhead—her short bob was prone to stick up in all directions—before kicking off the blankets and making her way to the door. Catalina stood outside the doorway, her deep brown eyes wide and her lips pinched with worry.

"What's wrong?" Margot asked.

"Derek's missing."

Margot stared mouth agape at the other woman. "What?"

"He's gone."

Margot pushed past the other woman and marched down the hall. The door to Derek's room was ajar. The bedclothes were a wrinkled mess, shoved to one side. She peered out the window. At least the storm had stopped raging. She tried to find any sign that he'd simply gone outside to shovel, but the snowdrifts on the front lawn and driveway were undisturbed.

"He was here a few hours ago," Margot muttered.

"How do you know?" Catalina's tone carried a note of accusation.

Margot realized the fact that she and not his wife knew of his late-night whereabouts, appeared suspect. Catalina didn't think there was anything Margot and Derek might have shared during duty, did she?

"He was having flashbacks in his sleep. Nightmares really. I heard him and woke him up," Margot replied.

Catalina's face fell and she slunk into the room and perched on the foot of the bed. "He won't tell me what's been going on. Do you know what he doesn't want to talk about?"

Margot sat beside her and placed a hand on her shoulder. "I do, but it's not my place to share it with you. He knows you're here for him. You need to be patient. The things he's seen and lost during his time overseas will take a lot of time to heal, if they ever do. And, I hope you don't think there is anything besides friendship between him and me. All he could do was talk about you when we were abroad. He was so excited that you'd agreed to marry him when he got home."

Catalina's shoulders relaxed a fraction. "Honestly, when he talked about you at church all the time, it worried me. He put you on a pedestal like you could do no wrong and you were perfect. He said it so much, everyone believed it."

"I'm far from perfect. I appreciate his support of my abilities, but I have to admit it surprised me to hear he'd been talking about me to everyone. I'm still unsure that's my place or purpose."

"Even if you're only half as good as he says, I think the church would do well under your leadership. We need someone from our generation who understands what it means to be a thirty-something these days. The issues we face are so very different from when our parents were our age."

Margot blushed at Catalina's praise, such as it was. The more she heard from the people around her, the more she thought perhaps it was worth a try to see if the church was the right place for her to go on her spiritual journey. She had to believe that

God was putting these circumstances in her path for a reason.

"Come on, maybe Derek just went for a walk or something," Margot suggested and stood up.

After retrieving her blouse from the guest room, they walked side by side downstairs and Margot allowed Catalina to lead her through to a different room, one that she'd not seen before. It looked like a library, the shelves piled high with carefully curated and preserved books, some were leather-bound. She plucked one off the shelf in a section devoted to taxidermy and flipped to the front page. It was a first edition. Derek was nowhere to be found.

"Is there somewhere else in the house he would go?"

"I mean, there's space in the basement but it's storage. We used to play hide and seek there when we were really little. Derek and I would hide for hours down there, pretending we were explorers. The things you think of as children," Catalina said with a sad smile.

"Can I ask you something?" Margot pressed as they made their way toward the back of the house and down a set of cement steps.

"Sure."

"Did you notice when Warren's behavior and temperament changed?" She had a suspicious feeling that Catalina would know the answer. The more information she could gather, the better chance she had of figuring out what had turned such a decent man into a monster. And maybe it could even help Sam find the responsible party, if Warren had been murdered.

"While Derek was away. It started slowly at first, I guess. Just sort of forgetful. Then he would get kind of grumpy and yell at people. Sometimes people who weren't even in the room. Then, he treated my mother like she was trash. It's been like that since Derek got home."

"This was around the time he was diagnosed with diabetes, right?"

"I guess so. He didn't like to talk about it. He hated to think he was less than perfect. Then again, it didn't stop him from thinking he could do things he shouldn't."

"What do you mean by that?"

Catalina stopped at the foot of the stairs, twisting the hem of her shirt between her fingers. "He would … never mind. Forget it."

"No, it's clearly weighing on you. Please, I'm here to listen. I promise, I'm really good at it."

Catalina glanced around her as if to make sure no one would hear her. "A few times, he made some…comments to me that weren't really appropriate. Sexual comments. My mother and Mary heard them and they both got upset. Then one time, he tried to grab me. I never told Derek. Please you can't tell him that."

"So, that's not what he and Warren were arguing about last night?"

"No. Derek's been having a rough time with adjusting back to civilian life and Warren thought it was an act. Like he thought because he'd gone off to war, he had to act wounded."

"I'm sorry you had to endure that. It sounds horrible. For everyone."

"Please don't tell Derek about the comments," Catalina repeated.

"I won't. You have my word."

Margot wasn't sure where her gut was leading her with this diabetes angle, but it felt like it was the right track. Still, she dropped the topic as they reached the basement door which sat ajar.

"When was the last time someone was down here?" Margot asked, noting the disturbed line of dust on the ground.

"Not in months."

Margot got in front of the other woman, letting some of her military training take over. She eased the door open more with her left shoulder, letting in some of the dim sunlight slanting through a high window on the far wall. The shaft of light was enough to illuminate Derek sitting in the middle of the room. He clutched something to his chest and rocked back and forth.

"Derek. It's Margot, can you hear me?" she called.

Derek didn't react. Perhaps he was sleepwalking. He wasn't whimpering or crying anymore, but his eyes appeared glassy and his skin was freezing. As she moved closer, Margot saw he was clutching a shirt tight to his chest. It was a few sizes too big for him. Perhaps one of Warren's shirts. Catalina rushed into the room and threw herself at her husband. He didn't react to the weight of her body against his. He continued clutching the shirt tightly.

"Derek, honey, it's me. It's Cat. Wake up!" She shook him.

He didn't react. Instead, he began mumbling under his breath. "I'm sorry. I'm sorry."

Margot needed to intervene and so she bent down in front of him. She gripped his hands and pulled them away from his chest. For the second time in only a few hours, she said, "Private Nesbit. Attention now, soldier."

Derek's head swiveled to the sound of Margot's voice. He blinked and looked at his surroundings. He relinquished his hold on the shirt and Margot's hands. "What's going on?"

"I think you were sleep-walking. Baby, you're so cold." Catalina pressed a hand to his forehead.

"I … the last thing I remember was going to sleep after the police left."

"You don't remember our conversation

this morning?" Margot stood to give him space.

"No. We talked?"

Margot nodded. "You were having flash-backs about Peter. Remember?"

Derek struggled to his feet, hampered in his effort by Catalina's weight. "I think it's coming back to me."

"Why do you have one of Uncle Warren's shirts?" Catalina pressed.

Derek glanced down at the fabric that was now covering his bare feet. "What? I don't remember getting it. I guess … I feel bad about arguing with him."

"We should get you cleaned up and into some warmer clothes," Catalina added.

"I still can't believe he's gone," Derek murmured, still confused.

They started up the cold cement steps and made a beeline to the kitchen where they found Mary pouring coffee grinds into the percolator. She looked like she hadn't slept well. She turned at the footsteps and gave them a tired smile.

"I hope I didn't wake you," she said.

"No. We were up," Margot answered. She nudged Derek. "You should go get cleaned up."

He nodded without a word and disappeared from view. Margot peered around, wondering where Rosalinda had gone. The kitchen looked no cleaner or tidier than it had the night before so she hadn't really done any cleaning in the middle of the night. *What was she doing down here then?*

"I'm not sure what we've got in the fridge, but you're welcome to whatever we have," Mary offered.

Margot started with a cup of coffee once it finished brewing. "I think the storm has stopped. If it's all right with you, I'll dig myself out and head home."

"We'd be happy to help," Mary said.

Before Margot could respond, her phone

rang from inside her pocket. She yanked it free and saw an unfamiliar number flashing on the screen. "Excuse me."

She stepped into the foyer before answering. "Hello?"

"Margot, it's Sam," her cousin said from the other end. She sounded about as awake as Margot felt.

"Oh, uh, morning." She sipped from the cup in her hand.

"Are you still at the Nesbit house?"

"Until I can dig my car out. Why?"

"Can you stick around for a while?"

"What's going on?"

Sam let out an exaggerated sigh. "We got preliminary results back. Warren's insulin levels were off the charts."

"He was diabetic and used injectable insulin for treatment." *That made sense, didn't it?* Then again, Sam wouldn't be calling if it were a usual circumstance.

"When I say off the charts, I mean he was overdosing on the stuff."

"Are you sure? It was still a new disease for him. Maybe he was trying to get the hang of the dosage."

"Maybe, but the ME said that the levels looked like they were from prolonged dosing."

"That's concerning."

"Exactly."

"What can I do?"

"Just keep folks calm. I don't know, give them spiritual guidance or help planning the funeral."

"That feels disingenuous."

"Just do what they expect of you given your profession."

Margot wasn't comfortable deceiving the Nesbits just to keep them occupied while Sam conducted her investigation. But she also couldn't deny that she wanted to dig deeper into the circumstances surrounding

Warren's death. If she had to assign motive to anyone, she worried Derek was a likely suspect. He clearly had issues with his uncle's reaction to his time overseas.

Still if Warren had been receiving higher doses of insulin for a long time, Derek couldn't have been the one responsible. The timeline didn't add up. Rosalinda and Catalina also had motive to want to put him in his place given his horrid treatment of them. But, did they have access to the medication or did he inject himself? And why had Mary failed to mention Warren's diagnosis to Sam? Margot needed an opportunity to look around the rest of the house while also keeping the family occupied. So, she would just have to agree to Sam's terms.

"Fine. I'll see if I can keep them occupied. Are you coming back over?"

"Yes. With another forensics team. Now that we know he had diabetes, we need to investigate the angle."

Margot ended the call, hoping no one else had heard her conversation. She tried to run over her responses to Sam's questions in her mind. Without the benefit of the context of Sam's statements, her answers didn't seem too out of the ordinary or obvious. When she returned to the kitchen, she found that Rosalinda had joined them and stood over the stove cooking French toast and pancakes.

"What would we do without Rosa," Mary said with a heavy sigh.

"If you don't mind," Margot said, "do you think I could use the bathroom and take a quick shower?"

"Of course. We'll save you breakfast."

"And I wanted to let you know if you need help with making arrangements for the funeral, I'm here to support you. Whatever you need." She waited to see if Mary would dismiss her offer in the same way she had the day before.

Mary gave Derek an approving glance.

"You were right about her. She will be perfect to lead the church."

Margot didn't respond to Mary's statement, using the distraction to backtrack up to the second floor. She moved down the hall to the bathroom and turned on the shower, feeling guilty for wasting the hot water. She then made her way down to the other end of the hall and into the master bedroom. She took in the large room with the heavy drapes and the thick covers in deep burgundy. It was an inviting space. She moved through the room, stopping first at the bedside table on the right. It bore a small mirror and reading light. She suspected this was Mary's side of the bed. Operating under that assumption, she moved to the other side of the bed and eased the drawer to the matching nightstand open, using the sleeve of her shirt to ensure she didn't leave any prints.

Margot expected to find syringes and vials of insulin in the drawer. It was empty.

Not even a comb or cell phone charger. *Where were they kept?* She moved back to Mary's side and pulled open the drawer. The syringes and insulin sat in neat rows. The syringes were blocked after a certain point, ensuring the needles would dispense the same amount of medication. She picked up the insulin bottle to compare the dosage to the syringe depth. As Sam had noted, the syringes were set to administer twice the recommended dose. *Why would Mary be giving him twice as much as prescribed?*

"What is going on?" she whispered to herself.

"Can I help you find something?" Mary asked from the doorway.

Margot let out a gasp of surprise. Quickly, she returned the vial to the drawer and closed it before turning back to face her hostess. "You scared me."

"I thought you were taking a shower."

"Yes. I was just wondering if there was any body wash."

"Not in the bedroom. I'll show you."

Margot's heart didn't stop racing until Mary had left her alone in the bathroom, the mirror above the sink thick with steam. Margot shed her clothing and stepped beneath the warm water. The shower had been a pretense to snoop around the house, but she could still use one. It gave her time to ponder why Mary would purposely overdose her husband's medication.

7

True to their word, the others had saved some breakfast for Margot. A plate of pancakes and French toast sat on the kitchen counter with a small container of maple syrup beside it. She picked up the plate and made her way into the dining room. Derek was the only one remaining from the group.

"Where's everyone else?" Margot asked.

"They went out to shovel. They figured you would want to get out of here."

Margot was a little surprised, because

Derek—who was always first to offer to do the chores everyone else complained about—had let others take up shovels. But he'd had a rough night. The dark circles under his eyes were even more pronounced, accenting the bruise. He was still in his pajamas. She could at least spare him the embarrassment of the police searching his home while he was indisposed.

"You should get dressed," she said.

"I'll keep you company while you eat."

"Really, it's fine."

His eyes narrowed. They'd spent enough time together that he knew when she wasn't telling him something. "What is it? What aren't you telling me?"

"The police need to come back and look at some more things. It would be better if you weren't in your pajamas when they arrive."

"How do you know they're coming back?"

"Officer Raymond called me. I think she still wants me here with everyone else, in case she has any more questions for all of us." Hmm … Like why Mary was the one dispensing Warren's insulin or what had caused those flakes around his mouth and the sweaty sheen on his body?

"Right. Of course, she called you. I forgot, you're related, aren't you?"

"That doesn't mean she'll do a less than professional job. I know my cousin. She's meticulous but fair. If something out of the ordinary happened to your uncle, she will figure it out."

"I have a bad feeling about all of this. I mean, I know I was gone for a while, but I can't wrap my head around why he acted so different toward everyone."

It was a good question. One to which she planned on finding an answer. "I can eat by myself. You really should go get cleaned up before they arrive."

He nodded and traipsed out of the dining room. This left Margot with a little time to snoop. She pulled up a search browser on her cell phone and typed in "insulin overdose symptoms."

Over two million hits populated, but the top result was enough for her. The symptoms described fit the change in Warren's personality. Catalina had noted Warren had become confused at first, and then irritable and anxious. Perhaps even the sweaty sheen resulted from the increased insulin being processed by his body. It still didn't explain why Mary would have doubled the dose. Did she intend to harm her husband?

Margot took a few bites of the French toast, but it had gone cold taking on an odd flavor. Perhaps the syrup had congealed too much. The front door scraped open and she could hear voices echoing in the foyer.

"I don't understand why you have to come back," Mary argued.

"Mrs. Nesbit, your husband died under unusual circumstances. I wouldn't be doing my job if I didn't investigate. Now please, let's go inside so we can talk."

"No. I didn't ask for the police to be involved."

Margot abandoned the plate and entered the kitchen to see a flushed Mary Nesbit bundled in a parka and snow boots. Catalina and Rosalinda weren't with them. Mary and Sam blocked the doorway and Margot's view out into the driveway.

"Is everything all right?" Margot tried to defuse the situation.

The bigger audience changed Mary's demeanor. She lowered her voice and put on a smile. "I'm so sorry. I didn't mean to shout. It's just such a trying time. I feel like she isn't allowing our family the space to grieve our loss."

Mary was good, Margot would give her that. She could turn on a dime and play the bereaved widow well. Margot needed to pass on the information she'd gleaned to Sam without giving herself away. As it stood, Margot wasn't sure Mary didn't already know she was snooping and had found the stash of syringes. Had Mary already moved them or disposed of them entirely?

"I'm sure Officer Raymond is aware of the painful time your family finds themselves in," Margot said, eyeing her cousin.

"I am," Sam agreed. "Mrs. Nesbit, I know this is an intrusion, but we're just following up on a few things. It won't take much time."

Sam motioned to someone behind Mary and a pair of jumpsuit-clad forensic technicians trudged into the house. They were polite enough to kick off the snow from their boots before heading deeper into the house.

One technician moved into the kitchen and bent beneath the sink, rummaging through bottles, stuffing them at random into a clear plastic bag.

"Why are you taking those?" This time, it was Rosalinda who was being argumentive.

"We can't disclose that at this time," Sam answered.

"And where did that other one go?" Mary questioned.

Margot assumed he'd gone up to the second floor in search of the medication. She needed to let Sam know what she'd found, but out of nowhere, her head spun and the world flashed in and out of focus. Heat raced up her body from her toes and her vision greyed out, sending panicked signals to her brain. *Oh God, what's happening?*

"Sam, can I talk to you for a moment?" Margot thought her words were clear. She couldn't be certain though, because they didn't resound in her ears. She grabbed for the counter, but couldn't see anything.

She didn't get a verbal response. Instead, when the world righted itself, she was sitting in the dining room in the chair that Derek had vacated. Sam knelt beside her with worry lines furrowing her forehead.

"You okay?"

"I'm sorry," Margot said, "I don't know what came over me. One minute I was fine and then suddenly, I felt so dizzy and my vision blacked out."

"Just sit and take deep breaths."

Margot shook her head. "You need to know something."

"Whatever it is can wait. I want to make sure you're okay."

"No, listen to me. You were right. Warren was being given excessive doses of insulin." She leaned in close for fear of being overheard. "Mary was doing it. I saw the syringes and the vials in her bedside table."

Sam worried her lower lip. "You shouldn't have been snooping like that, Margot. You could have gotten hurt."

Margot wasn't sure if Mary had tried to sideline her with breakfast. She'd had plenty of opportunity to drug the food while Margot showered. But the dizziness didn't seem to correlate with an isolated instance of increased insulin. And would it even have the same effect if she ingested it?

Sam reached for a radio on her belt and held to her mouth. "Ben, check the master bedroom." She paused, eyeing Margot for more information.

"It should be on the righthand side when you enter the room."

"Righthand side."

"Copy that," Ben's voice crackled through the radio.

Margot looked up when someone set a glass of water in front of her. A slight panic spiked her heart rate, but she relaxed a fraction when she saw Catalina. "Here. You look like you could use it."

Margot gave a weak smile and took a small sip from the glass. Nothing tasted off and she took the chance, downing it in two big swallows.

"If you'll excuse me," Catalina said, "I should see where Derek went. He'll want to know what's going on."

Margot doubted he was unaware of the intruders disassembling his home, but neither Margot nor Sam stopped her. Margot turned back to Sam. "What are they looking for in the kitchen?"

"I can't tell you, Margot. You know that."

Margot cocked her head to one side. "I'm not asking for anything specific. I'm just curious. And I helped you out with the insulin. You shouldn't have told me about that either."

"You're right, I shouldn't have."

"But you did. Whether or not you like it, we're both invested in this. You want to find out the truth for your professional reputation. I want to ensure that this family gets the healing it needs. And I can't help them if I don't know what they need healing from."

Sam let out a huff. "Fine. The ME found unusual chemicals in his bloodwork."

"Would it explain the flakes around his mouth and the sheen on his skin when he died?"

"You saw that?"

Margot gave her cousin a knowing look. "I may be a servant of God but the Lord gave me eyes to see. Besides I can be rather observant when I want to be."

"Look, I'm sorry you got caught up in this mess," Sam said.

"It isn't anything you did. I accepted the dinner invitation. None of us expected it would end in the death of one of Port Marie's wealthier pillars of the community."

"Officer Raymond, there's nothing here," Ben's voice echoed over the radio still clutched in Sam's hand.

"She must have gotten rid of it after I found it," Margot muttered.

"Sounds like I better have another little chat with Mrs. Nesbit," Sam said with a resigned expression.

Margot waved her cousin onward. "Go. I'll be fine."

She wanted to believe Mary hadn't deliberately poisoned her husband, but Mary's behavior didn't project innocence. Feeling her strength return, Margot got to her feet and made a loop through the back of the house, coming around to the foyer just as Sam cornered Mary in the kitchen. Rosalinda, Derek and Catalina were gone. A sense of foreboding wrapped around Margot's shoulders like a cloak. There was something she was missing in all of this. It was staring her right in the face, but she couldn't see it.

8

Margot should have known it would all come back to the monstrous wild cats guarding the entryway to the second floor. She hadn't asked about them, but she should have questioned why they were there and where they came from.

Derek marched down the staircase alone and spotted Margot staring up at the lioness.

"Are you okay?" he asked.

"I never asked. Where did these come from? They don't seem like the sort of thing your uncle would display. I mean, I would have thought him to be against poaching."

"To be honest, I think his father killed them on a safari or something decades ago. The house belonged to him. Uncle Warren inherited it when he died. It was just too much work to get rid of them."

"Don't they creep you out a little?"

Derek laughed, the first happy sound she'd heard in two days. "When I was a little kid, I was always afraid they would come to life and eat me. I guess after a while, you almost forget they're even here."

She understood his childhood fear. Margot stepped up closer to the lioness. "They're kept in pristine condition."

"Oh yeah. The one thing Uncle Warren insisted upon was that they always look their best."

"How would he do that?"

"Oh, Uncle Warren did nothing. He delegated the task to other people."

She ran her finger along the lioness's muzzle. Her finger came away greasy with that same odd sheen Warren's body had taken on. Little flakes caught up in the air currents dusted her palm. They were just like the flakes around Warren's mouth. That explained why the forensic team collected chemicals from the kitchen.

Another piece of the puzzle took shape in Margot's mind, but it only complicated the narrative she'd been constructing. She still didn't know why Mary would overdose her husband on insulin. Perhaps, though, whoever was made to clean the lions had a reason to poison Warren, too.

"Who cleaned them?"

"Rosalinda. Why?"

"No reason." *Not one I can share with you, at least not yet.* She didn't want to deceive him, but she wasn't ready to add more pain to what he already carried.

"What exactly are you accusing me of,

Officer?" Mary's voice boomed throughout the first floor.

"I'm not accusing you of anything, Mrs. Nesbit. I asked you a simple question. Did your husband administer his own medication?"

Derek cleared his throat. "I should go see to that."

Margot didn't stop him. She had other things on her mind like how someone might know the cleaner used on the lions could be harmful to humans. She made her way to the library, the book she'd examined the day before flashing in her mind.

The space seemed cavernous when she entered it this time. The shelves still housed immaculately-kept volumes, except there was an obvious gap in the taxidermy section. The book she'd examined was missing. Margot guessed the shelf was about shoulder height for both Rosalinda and her daughter. Just because Rosalinda was responsible for cleaning the lions didn't mean someone else in the house couldn't have gotten their hands on the chemicals and used them against Warren. By all accounts, he'd turned his anger toward both Catalina and her mother. Derek had access, too, but Margot refused to believe the man with whom she'd shared a tragic bond with would frame his mother-in-law. If Catalina was to be believed, he didn't know about Warren's sexual advances towards his new wife. That still left two suspects.

"You aren't taking my aunt anywhere," Derek's voice rang out.

Margot abandoned her book search and returned to the kitchen. Sam placed handcuffs around Mary's wrists.

"She didn't do anything," Derek continued to protest.

"If she would tell us where the insulin syringes are, we wouldn't have to do this," Sam answered.

Derek's eyes widened as he looked at his aunt. "Tell them where they are, Aunt Mary. Just tell them."

Mary shook her head. "I can't."

"Just tell them," he begged, his voice skyrocketing into falsetto.

"Mary," Margot said in a calm tone. She hoped it would have the effect of bringing everyone's emotions down to a more reasonable level. "I don't think you meant to hurt Warren. Please, just tell Officer Raymond what you know. The truth is always better."

Tears sparkled in Mary's eyes as she looked at her nephew. "You left us. We'd given you so much and you left us. It broke our hearts."

"I served my country. Something he never appreciated." Anger lowered Derek's tone to a bass.

"After a while, we adjusted," Mary said. "We still had Rosalinda and Catalina, but it wasn't the same. And then he got sick with the diabetes. I thought, I could at least take care of him. But he insisted he could do it himself. I wanted him to need me. I wanted *someone* to need me."

"So, you gave him more insulin than he needed," Sam prompted.

"He had trouble getting the right amount to begin with. I begged him to let me draw it for him. He could inject himself. So, he let me."

"Were you aware that his change in behavior and personality were because of the increased dosage you were giving him?" Margot's tone was soft, non-accusatory.

"No. I didn't know."

"You're the reason he became such a miserable excuse for a man?" Derek growled.

"I wanted him to need me," she repeated, tears staining her cheeks.

"Mary Ellen Nesbit, you are under arrest for the murder of Warren Nesbit. You have the right to remain silent, anything you say can and will be used against you in a court of law. You have the right to an attorney. If you cannot afford one, one will be provided to you. Do you understand these rights as I have read them to you?" Sam said.

"Yes," Mary mumbled before Sam led her out of the house, leaving Margot and Derek to watch in silence.

9

The gravity of Mary's actions settled over the space, sending Derek collapsing to his knees. Hoping to comfort him, Margot took a step toward him, but he recoiled before she even made contact.

"I'm so sorry," she said, keeping her distance.

"I should have known something was wrong," he mumbled.

"You were gone. You couldn't have known."

He looked around the kitchen. She didn't know what he hoped to find. Silence fell again between them and Margot waited. There was still something that made no sense. *What about the chemicals?* Had it been a misdirection or was there something else amiss in all of this?

"I have to tell Catalina," Derek announced.

Bringing up the chemicals seemed like a cruel thing to do to her friend. He'd just lost both parental figures in his life in the span of a day. But, if Mary's actions hadn't been the only factor in Warren's death, shouldn't he know the truth? Shouldn't they all know the truth?

"How can I help?" Margot asked. Keeping the chemical knowledge to herself until she had definite answers seemed safer.

"I… I don't know. I said so many horrible things to him. I thought he'd just become a crotchety old man in my absence. But it was out of his control. It was all her doing."

"You have every right to be angry with her," Margot said.

He looked at her and anger flushed his cheeks. "Is this where you tell me to forgive her because that's what God would want me to do?"

"Listen, someday, yes, if you can find it in your heart to forgive her, you should. But it is human nature to harbor anger. We aren't perfect, that's sort of the point. We have flaws and we make mistakes. Now, I can't speak for your aunt, but it seemed like she acted out of a need that wasn't being fulfilled in her marriage. That isn't on you."

"I'll be the laughingstock of the town. Maybe it's better if Cat and I go away for good after our honeymoon."

"Go where?"

"We're taking a honeymoon to the Bahamas and we're leaving soon—we already have the boarding passes. Just to get away. Be in the sun and sand for a while, and then we'd come back. But after this, I don't think I can show my face around here. Everyone knows our family. They respected us and looked up to us."

"And they listened when you touted the abilities of a lowly Army Chaplain," she reminded him.

His anger ebbed a little. "If they've got half a brain they'll listen. You deserve to have your own congregation and this town is lacking in younger leadership."

"I appreciate your vote of confidence, I do. And if you feel you need a fresh start after all that's happened, I would understand. But don't disappear forever, okay? You aren't the only one who needs a friendly ear from time to time."

"I won't ghost you, Chaplain," he said with a fleeting smile.

"Come on. Let's find your wife and mother-in-law and break the news."

Derek refused her help as he got to his feet. They checked the entire first floor but the other two women were nowhere to be found. They tried upstairs and found them sitting in Catalina's bedroom. Margot spotted the boarding passes sitting in an envelope on the dresser. *Did the police find the tickets and jump to the wrong conclusion?*

"What's going on? Have the police left?" Catalina asked.

Margot placed a comforting hand on Derek's shoulder, urging him to break the news.

He cleared his throat a few times, then said, "They arrested Aunt Mary."

"What? Why? That's ridiculous. She wouldn't have done anything," Catalina protested.

Derek hung his head. "She was giving him too much insulin. He was overdosing on the stuff. The police think that's why he was acting so irritably and everything. She made him like this."

"Why would she do that?" Rosalinda's voice was timid.

"We can't speak to her motives. Although from what she said to Officer Raymond when they took her into custody, she was trying to fill her own need to be needed," Margot answered, keeping Derek from having to explain.

"I can't believe I never noticed anything," Catalina murmured, sinking back on the bed.

Derek joined her and wrapped his arm around her shoulders, pulling her close. "None of us did. I think maybe after we take our honeymoon, we should think about moving."

Awkward silence fell over the group of four. Margot knew she should leave them to their private conversation, but her instincts kept her there.

"But Port Marie is our home," Catalina argued.

"It used to be. But after this, how can we face everyone? We didn't do anything wrong, but that doesn't mean they won't still talk about us. You know the people here. They love to gossip and spread conspiracy theories."

He wasn't wrong. Port Marie wasn't immune to idle gossip and the town had its share of skeletons in its collective closet. Catalina glanced at her mother, who remained quiet and contemplative.

"Mami, you'd come with us, right?"

Rosalinda looked up, startled by her daughter's question. "Yes, *mija*." She looked around the room. "Why would I stay here. I am not needed anymore."

It was Margot's turn to clear her throat.

"I'll leave you all for now. You have my number. Please call if you need anything—help with the funeral, or just someone to lean on. I want you to know I'm here for you."

Derek offered his hand. "Thank you. I know you didn't sign up for any of this when you came for dinner."

"Sometimes we don't know where we're needed until we find ourselves there."

She headed downstairs, donned her coat, and braved the wintry landscape outside. It appeared Catalina and Rosalinda had dug out her car and had even cleaned it off. Margot climbed in and started the engine, cranking the heater to full blast. She stayed put until a steady stream of warm air caressed her face and fogged the interior of the windshield. Margot wasn't sure where to go now. She had no way to prove whether the cleaning chemicals had been in Warren's system. Sam wouldn't be thrilled to see her, especially if Margot intended to poke holes in the neatly wrapped up case. She also knew her cousin would want the truth and see justice done, even if that meant the case took an unexpected twist.

10

"I'm sorry, Officer Raymond is off duty. You can speak to one of our other officers," the dispatcher said at the front desk.

His nameplate read *Officer Weiss*, so Margot said, "I'm sorry to have bothered you, Officer Weiss. But this is an issue that I need to discuss with Officer Raymond. It concerns a case she's investigating."

The older man eyed her warily. "I'll see if I can get a hold of her. But she might not answer. She takes her time off seriously."

"I don't doubt it. If you could just tell her that Margot is asking for her and it's related to the case."

"Care to be more specific?" he asked.

"She'll know what I'm referencing." If this officer wasn't aware of Mary Ellen Nesbit being brought in for killing her husband, Margot wouldn't feed into the rumor mill.

"Take a seat over there. I'll let you know if I can get ahold of her."

"Thank you so much for your help." Margot took a seat in one of the hard-backed plastic chairs in the waiting area.

The military had trained her to put up with a whole host of situations. Waiting in a small police precinct was nothing compared to most of them. Besides, it would give her a chance to people watch. It was a hobby she'd developed while serving overseas. She could learn a lot about a person just by watching them in their environment.

"Yeah, Officer Raymond, I'm sorry to disturb you during your day off but I've got a Margot here. She says she needs to talk to you about a case you're working. She wouldn't say which case. I can tell her to come back another"—he held the receiver to his shoulder, blocking the speaker with one hand. "Ma'am, she's asking to speak with you directly."

"Thank you." Margot stood and accepted the phone. "Hi, Sam."

"What is it?"

Margot turned her back to the dispatcher. "It would be better if we could meet in person to discuss this."

"I'm not sure what there is to discuss. Case is closed."

"I think you're wrong. Or at least, you're missing something."

"I don't tell you how to minister to people. Don't tell me how to do police work. Got it?" Her cousin's tone stung.

"I'm not trying to. But there's a piece of

this you haven't fully considered. You want to make sure everything you have is accurate, don't you?"

"Fine. But I'm not coming back in. It's my day off."

"I can come to you," Margot offered.

"I'll give you the address."

Margot smiled. "You haven't moved in four years. You haven't even changed your phone number."

"Oh, right."

"I'll be right over." She handed the receiver back to Officer Weiss. "Thank you."

She zipped up her coat and retreated to her car, intent on making one detour before she met up with Sam. Bringing a peace offering wouldn't be a bad thing.

SHE ARRIVED fifteen minutes later with a hot coffee for them both. Even a minister of the

Lord needed a pick-me-up now and again. And Margot had to admit that the coffee stateside was far superior to the watered-down imitation served on base.

When Margot knocked, Sam opened the door dressed in baggy sweatpants and a sweatshirt with Port Marie's police emblem emblazoned on the front.

"I come bearing gifts." Margot held out one of the travel cups.

Sam accepted it and ushered Margot inside. The house looked the same as the last time Margot had been here. She'd helped Sam move in after she rented the place. She had fond memories of the pair of them staying awake until the early hours of the morning, chatting and sharing their plans for their lives. It was surprising how much had gone to plan for them both. And what hadn't. Margot had always assumed her cousin would settle down and marry long before Margot did. Yet, they were both still single.

"This place hasn't changed," Margot said, as they moved into the living room with its inviting stucco fireplace and loveseat.

"Well, I own the place outright now."

Margot's jaw dropped. "You bought it? When?"

Sam shrugged one shoulder. "A year ago. But you didn't come over to talk about the fact I'm a home owner now."

"No, I didn't." Margot set her coffee on the coffee table in front of the loveseat. "I know you were looking at the cleaning chemicals at the house and you wouldn't tell me why."

"I can't discuss parts of my investigation with a civilian. You get that, right?"

"I do. But I can't shake this feeling that there's something to it."

"Look, we have the killer. She confessed and we know how she did it."

"Did the medical examiner tell you definitively that it was just an insulin overdose? I mean, would that even be enough to kill someone?"

"We are still waiting on a more detailed report. What are you getting at?"said Sam starting to get irritated.

Time to put all of her cards on the table and hope Sam took the leap of faith with her. "We both know about the flakes on his body. And I don't know but this morning when I was eating, I felt sick. Like maybe someone put something in the food."

"How are either of those things connected?"

"You said there were some odd chemicals in his blood. I noticed the same flakes on the lions by the entryway. Derek told me that Rosalinda cleans them. She's the only one. Plus, there was a book in the library on taxidermy that went missing."

"So what, you think Mary knew that and used it, too? Why would she do that?"

"I don't know why Mary would do that."

She knew Rosalinda had at least one reason motivating her. Maybe Margot could get the other woman to confess before she brought Sam into it. "You know what? I think I'm letting this all get to me. You're right. I'm not the investigator here. I'll stay in my lane. Enjoy the coffee."

Margot retrieved her cup and was halfway to the front door before Sam called out to her. "I'm sorry we had to reconnect like this. But I'm glad we did. I hope you know that."

Margot turned and gave her cousin a smile. "I'm glad, too. I've missed you."

Now, if she could secure the final piece of this puzzle, maybe things would feel right again.

11

Margot wasn't sure where she would find the answers she was looking for. So, she let God lead her, and she ended up at the church.

It was her first time at the church since she'd been home. God had led her to the right place, because she could use the quiet to reflect on the situation. The emptiness would also afford her a chance to explore the other areas added onto the original church building when the town had deemed it an interfaith space. She wandered from the narthex to the prayer room. A handful of prayer rugs were laid out ready for use. A stack of others sat piled high off to one side. The mid-afternoon sunlight dappled the wooden floor through a high window. She'd known a few soldiers who practiced Islam and she had always found their time for prayer soothing. She hadn't been able to learn all of the prayers, but she'd committed to learning enough to share in their worship.

Next, she made her way to the east hall that now served as the synagogue. It appeared empty; only a few chairs scattered through the space signaled that anyone had been inside in a while. She could see a fine coating of dust covering the space. Perhaps they'd used the sanctuary instead. It was a far more inviting atmosphere. She wound her way back to that part of the church, expecting it still to be vacant.

A lone figure sat up at the front near the pulpit.

From this distance, Margot couldn't discern their identity. She wanted to give whoever it was their privacy. The sound of her footsteps on the creaky stairs leading in from of the narthex drew the other occupant's attention. When the person turned, Margot recognized Rosalinda's dark eyes and greying temples, but she appeared pale even with her cinnamon colored skin.

"I didn't mean to disturb you," Margot said.

"It is okay." Rosalinda continued to gaze back at Margot, almost inviting her to close the distance and join her.

"Do you mind if I join you?'

Rosalinda shook her head and patted the pew beside her. Margot started down the center aisle, taking her time, formulating a way she could broach the subject without appearing accusatory.

"It's been a long few days, hasn't it?"

Margot said when she settled in beside the older woman.

"Yes." Rosalinda opened her mouth to say more, but stopped.

"I'm so sorry that you're out of a job," Margot said.

Rosalinda fiddled with a few strands of loose hair. "I do not know that it matters."

"Why would you say that?" Margot asked as gently as possible.

Rosalinda kneaded her hands together, not making eye contact. Instead, she turned her attention to the pulpit and the image of Christ on the cross. If she needed to make her confession to Christ, so be it. In a voice so quiet it sounded like a sigh, she whispered, "I did something."

"I'm here to listen." Margot didn't want to lull the woman into a false sense of safety, but she was there to listen to whatever had prompted Rosalinda's change of heart.

"When Derek told us, what Mary did…it made me angry."

"Angry? Because you had no job?"

Rosalinda shook her head. "Angry because I…did something I can't take back."

"What did you do?"

"Mr. Nesbit was always particular. He told me to clean the lions every day." Anger clouded her facial features and her lips pursed. "He had given me so much that I put up with it. But then he became mean. He said I would do it wrong. It made him angry. He even hit me few times."

"I'm so sorry that happened. He had no right to do that."

She sighed. "It was because of what Mary did to him. If she let him be, he would not have become so angry and hateful. He would not have tried to hurt me or my daughter while her husband was away." She turned to look at Margot. "You know he said things no man should say to a woman who is engaged?"

Margot nodded. Rosalinda danced around the actual truth of what she'd done. As awful as her actions were, Margot grew frustrated with the runaround. "If there's something else you want to tell me, you know you can."

"You will tell the police lady."

"There is a clergy congregant privilege which means our conversation is confidential, but I think you would feel better if you came clean."

"I mixed some of the cleaner with his drinks. I read it could be harmful. I did not mean to kill him. I only wanted to make him stop. I did not know it would do that."

Margot wanted to believe her statement. The sadness that now showed on the woman's face and the unshed tears in her eyes showed it was the truth. Just like Mary, she hadn't meant to kill him. It was likely a combination of the insulin overdose and the cleaner that were the true culprits.

"You had no idea that Mary was poisoning him, too?"

"No. I did not know what she did. I swear to God."

"And she didn't know what you were doing," Margot muttered mostly to herself.

"I do not think so. No."

Margot let out a long breath and turned to face the image of Christ. She'd found out the truth about Warren's death. It hadn't been intentional on either of the women's part and they hadn't acted together. There was no conspiracy. With enough time, the medical examiner could determine how much each woman contributed to Warren's demise. What that would mean for their futures was still up in the air.

"I won't tell the police what you've told me here today. But, again, I think you would feel better if you told them what happened."

"I will go to jail."

"Possibly. I can't say for certain what will happen. I don't think anyone can. You did what you did to protect yourself and your daughter, which is an admirable thing. You went about it the wrong way but I'm sure they will take that into consideration. I'll go with you to the police station if you want. And I can also go with you when you tell Catalina the truth."

"This will break my Catalina's heart. I can't tell her."

"You can't just vanish from her life. She needs to know the truth so she and Derek can begin the process of healing. Please, don't keep this burden on yourself."

"I am scared."

"I know. But you aren't alone in this. I promise. I'll go with you."

She nodded and reached out for Margot's hand. Rosalinda faltered as she stood. Margot caught her, letting the older woman place her weight more fully on Margot's shoulders. They took their time walking out of the church and to Margot's car. The ride back to the Nesbit house was silent, but Margot didn't mind. She let Rosalinda build up the courage to come clean to her daughter and son-in-law.

Margot knocked on the front door, feeling it better to announce their presence given the news they were about to impart.

"Mami, why are you knocking?" Catalina asked upon answering the door.

"I need to talk to you, *mija*. Is Derek here?"

"He's down in the basement. He's been going through Warren's things. Why?"

"You should get him," Margot said.

Catalina remained in the doorway, color draining from her face. "What is going on? Just tell me."

"It's better if we come inside. Please," Margot prodded.

"Mami?" Catalina asked.

"Listen to her,' Rosalinda replied.

Catalina stepped back and let them inside. Margot held tight to Rosalinda's hand as they made their way into the library.

"I'll get Derek," Catalina said, her tone flat. Margot supposed she was preparing for the worst. *Had she put two and two together about the fact the forensic team was looking at cleaning supplies?*

Derek and Catalina returned a few moments later. He looked tired and grimy, but attentive. Catalina was still pale and she held tight to her husband's hand.

"You're back, Chaplain," Derek said. "What's going on?"

"Rosalinda needs to share something with you both," Margot replied, squeezing Rosalinda's hand tight.

"I can't come with you when you go away," Rosalinda began.

"Of course, you can. We aren't going to

just leave you here. You don't have to worry about that. Our trip is only for ten days. We'll be back before you know it," Catalina argued.

"No, *mija*. I won't be going with you because I have to stay here."

"I don't understand. Why?" Derek asked.

Rosalinda's tears fell, carving tracks along her cheeks. "Because I have to go to the police station. I did something bad to Mr. Nesbit. I have to tell them what I did."

Derek frowned. "You didn't do anything, Rosa. Aunt Mary hurt him. She's the reason he's dead."

"No. I hurt him, too. He treated me so bad, I got angry. I wanted him to stop so I tried to make him sick. I never meant to kill him. I don't think I would have killed him on my own, not even as an accident. Maybe we both did it without meaning to. But I can't live with it. I have to tell the truth."

"You can't do that. You'll go to jail. I won't let you," Catalina erupted.

"It isn't up to you," Margot said in a gentle voice. "Rosalinda decided to confess to the police, to take responsibility for her part in what happened. She's doing the honorable thing."

"Why would you do that? Why wouldn't you tell me?" Catalina broke down, tears marring her cheeks too.

"I was trying to protect you. To protect us both. It is what a parent does for a child. I will bear this burden on my own shoulders. You will live your life. You two have so much ahead of you."

"I can't do this without you, Mami."

Derek remained quiet and Margot watched him, trying to gauge his reaction. He'd already suffered a blow by finding out his aunt—his mother figure—had been the reason he'd lost his father figure, no matter how difficult their relationship had become.

Now, he had to be a rock for his wife who was suffering the same blow. It was a horrible situation and she was at a loss for how to make it better.

"Rosalinda, if you want me to go to the station with you, I'll do that," Margot offered again.

Rosalinda shook her head. "Thank you. You have been very kind to us these last few days when you did not have to be." She looked to her daughter and son-in-law. "Lean on each other. Lean on her, even if you do not make this place your home anymore. You have someone here who will understand your loss and your pain and will not judge you for your anger."

"I am really sorry for everything that's happened," Margot whispered before leaving them to sort out their own affairs.

1 2

---

month had passed since Warren Nesbit's death. A well-attended service was held at the church and a judge allowed both Rosalinda and Mary to attend. Their children had been good enough to put on a show of a united, though grieving, front during the service. Privately, Margot knew, they were hurting and angry. Sam let Margot know that the medical examiner determined a lethal combination of the insulin and the cleaner had stopped Warren's heart. It wasn't possible to tell which woman was more at fault and they'd both agreed to private plea deals. They would each serve reduced sentences.

Rumors swirled about the circumstances of Warren's passing and the fact that the Nesbit home was now for sale. Derek and Catalina were moving to Maine and had placed a down payment on a small house.

"You look ready," Reverend Hawley said from behind Margot.

She turned to look at him and smiled. Today was her first day as the new minister of Port Marie's interfaith church. She'd let Derek's praise fuel the congregation into calling her to serve them and she'd found a welcoming sea of faces when she stood at the pulpit. She'd spent a long time preparing for this week's sermon. It seemed she'd found her purpose after all.

"I hope so. It's been a while since I've had to prepare a sermon." She smoothed the vestments around her neck.

"You're going to do fine. You've been pre-paring for this, for a very long time. The people out there are waiting for you to share your wisdom."

"I'm glad you're here. I'm not sure I could get through today without seeing your face in the congregation."

"Just focus on me if it helps."

"It will. Thank you!"

He patted her on the arm and left her to gather her notes. She studied the points she wanted to highlight. The community needed to remember that even when Daniel entered the lion's den, God looked out for him and brought him out of danger un-harmed. Port Marie would come through this trying time stronger. So would Derek and Catalina.

Margot took a few steadying breaths be-fore she moved behind the pulpit. Her jaw went slack at the packed house. She spotted a few yarmulkes and hijabs in the crowd. Sitting right in the front row were two faces she hadn't expected to see.

Derek and Catalina.

Reverend Hawley sat two rows back and to their left. She didn't need to preach to him when she could speak to the people who needed to hear her message the most. Margot smiled out at the waiting faces and gave the cue to the organist to begin the prelude and first hymn. She liked that they changed up the musical selections to represent different faiths. Everyone returned to their seats and Margot stepped up to the microphone.

"Good morning, everyone. I'm so glad to see so many people here today. You really know how to make a person feel welcome. Port Marie has been my home my entire life but it wasn't until I went away for a while that I realized just how much it meant to call it home. I am grateful that you and God have called me to serve as your minister. I know that our community suffered a loss. But, together, we will weather this storm and come out the other side stronger."

When she made direct eye contact with Derek, he gave her an encouraging smile.

She continued, "Some of you may know that I served as a Chaplain in the Army and did a tour of duty overseas. In my time there, we witnessed a lot of strife and struggle. But the story of Daniel and the lion's den reminds us that even in the most perilous of situations, we can come out stronger if we have faith in God's guiding force. I hope we can all remember this important message as we move forward together."

Derek gave a small nod of understanding and her day was complete. She had touched one person, which was her goal in her ministry. Impacting one life can multiply and she was counting on that feeling spreading.

The rest of the service passed in a blur and before she knew it, Margot stood at the entrance to the fellowship hall, shaking hands and greeting faces both old and new. She waited, scanning the crowd for Derek and Catalina. They finally made their way to the front of the line.

"Good sermon, Reverend," Derek said.

"No Chaplain?" she teased.

"Well, you'll always be Chaplain to me, but you're serving a wider congregation than just our unit now."

"I have to admit it surprised me seeing the two of you here today. Happy, but surprised."

"We wouldn't miss your first sermon," Derek replied.

"How are you holding up?"

"We're taking it day by day," Catalina replied, holding tight to her husband's arm.

"We haven't been to see them," Derek said, without prompting.

"Give it time," Margot answered. She eyed the growing line behind them and gave them a sad smile. "Come find me later. I'm happy to chat."

"Thanks."

They melted into the crowd within the fellowship hall, leaving Margot to greet more congregants. Sam made her way down the stairs and stopped in front of Margot. Margot was about to offer a handshake to her cousin when Sam pulled her into a tight hug. The rest of the people around them gave them space.

"What was that for?" Margot asked.

"I should have done it a while ago. I know I was territorial with the whole investigation thing, but I don't think I would have gotten the whole truth without you."

"You didn't need me. I just pointed out a couple things. You did all the hard work."

Sam shook her head. "This was my first homicide," she confided.

"I couldn't tell," Margot replied.

"Thanks."

"You know, if you need to talk about any-thing, even if it's just silly stuff, I'm here." Having Sam back in her life brought Margot a deeper sense of connection to her home-town and her family, a lightness she hadn't felt since before her deployment.

"I will take you up on that." Sam looked at the gathered masses. "I hope everyone can take what you said today to heart."

"With time, everyone will move forward. They won't forget what happened, but they'll learn to forgive."

Margot truly believed that her little town would rebound from the loss of one of its more prominent figures. She would settle in to her new role and do what she could to help the healing process. She only prayed that such heartbreak wouldn't strike again anytime soon.

THE SACRIFICIAL LAMB

The Sacrificial Lamb

S.E. BIGLOW

 Created with Vellum

1

Winter was slow to leave the tiny town of Port Marie. Freezing temperatures and record snowfalls lingered into mid-March. Sitting in her office, Margot Quade looked outside. She could see the cold beginning to thaw and the tiniest shoots of new growth breaking the surface of the ground. The new life emerging reminded her that everything had its time. Only a few short months ago, she'd been called to serve her hometown's interfaith congregation as a minister. Finding her place again filled the void left by the end of her military service.

Coming home hadn't been as easy as she'd hoped. Warren Nesbit's murder became another black mark in the town's tragic history. Even if the gossip hadn't ignited as it sometimes did, Derek and Catalina Nesbit had uprooted their lives to get away from the reminder. There had been no trial. Both of Warren's killers had taken plea deals and were serving reduced sentences in a minimum-security facility upstate.

Margot looked up from making notes for next Sunday's sermon to see an email from Derek. He'd promised to stay in touch despite everything and he'd stayed true to his word. Just as she was about to open the message, a sharp knock on her office door made her wait.

Pedro Sanchez—the new custodian she'd hired—poked his head into the office. He was fresh out of college and eager to do a good day's work.

"Sorry to interrupt," he apologized.

Margot waved him into the room. "I think I need the distraction. What can I do for you?"

"Well, I was down in the basement to make sure everything was okay. You know, the electrical panels and boiler and everything. I think there's been some water damage from all the snow."

Margot wasn't surprised. The building itself was relatively old and could use a bit of a renovation. In fact, the combined congregations had agreed to help fund such a project once winter ended.

"Let's go take a look." She let him lead the way through the sanctuary and down two flights of stairs to the basement. She doubted anyone, but the custodian had paid a visit until now.

"I noticed a weird smell earlier, too,"

Pedro said when they arrived at their destination.

Margot inhaled, trying to catch a hint of whatever had drawn his attention, but she couldn't pick anything out. Pedro entered first, flicking the light on and casting the small room with a yellow glow. The basement was a cramped room with a pair of support beams in the middle. The electrical panel and boiler were housed along the far-left wall. Stacks of extra metal chairs leaned against the right wall. A handful of boxes sat against the wall directly in front of her. Margot saw dark stains on the floor where it met the far wall. Maybe Pedro was right and there had been damage from the storms given the high snow drifts and poor drainage around the building's foundation.

"You smell that?" he asked.

Margot inhaled again, closing her eyes this time to let her body focus on her sense of smell. She could pick out some general must and dampness common in basements after winter. She exhaled through her mouth and took another breath.

There, something putrid. Faint at first, the stench started to build as she walked deeper into the room.

"I do. I think it's coming from that wall." She pointed directly ahead.

"That's what I thought."

"I don't think this is just water damage from the snow storms," she said as they shoved the boxes out of the way.

The plaster wall had been painted beige. Even in the dim light, Margot spotted uneven color in a couple places.

She turned to Pedro. "Can you get some flashlights? The paint here looks a little off but it could just be the poor lighting."

"Sure thing." Pedro disappeared back upstairs, leaving Margot alone in the space.

She stepped up to the wall and ran her fingers over the paint. Despite the fact some parts looked more faded than other sections, it all felt coarse from the plaster. She tapped her knuckles on part of the wall that appeared newer. She moved her hand along the wall from left to right, her hand striking what sounded like a hollow space. *That's odd.*

"Pedro, you might want to grab a hammer while you're at it," she yelled up to him.

She didn't get a response, but assumed he heard her suggestion. She took another step along the wall. The paint looked older, as if it bore the original coat.

"Light and a hammer," Pedro announced from behind her a moment later.

He set a heavy sledge hammer down against one of the boxes and flipped on a camping lantern. It cast a stronger, orange glow along the wall and confirmed Margot's suspicion that there were different coats of paint.

"You're right, it looks like someone painted over parts of the wall," Pedro agreed.

"This spot here is hollow," she said, pointing to the swatch of newer paint. She wasn't an expert, but she figured even the newer coats were still old. Moving to the older section of paint, she knocked on the wall again, finding the same hollow sound. "It's hollow here, too."

"You think somebody just did a bad job insulating the walls?" Pedro asked.

"I don't know, but I have a feeling there's something back there. The smell has to be coming from it."

"What do you think it is?" His eyes sparkled in the light.

She wasn't as eager as her young friend to find out the answer to that question. A host of things could be hidden in a church built in the late 1800s. Anything with that kind of smell wouldn't be classified as a "good" thing. "I don't know. Be careful with that hammer though. We don't want to take the whole wall out. It's load bearing."

He hefted the hammer over his shoulder. "Don't worry, I got this."

Margot appreciated his confidence, but took a few steps back to give him a wide berth. She should have asked if he'd used a sledge hammer before. He squared up to the newer patch of wall and took a batter's stance, gripping the hammer with both hands. He took a practice swing, giving the wall a gentle tap where he intended to hit. On the next swing he put more force behind it and the wall cracked, kicking up dust. He coughed, but took another swing. This time, the chunk of wall he'd been aiming for crumbled to his feet.

"What do you see?" she asked as the dust and grime settled.

Pedro picked up the lantern and held it aloft. To his credit, he didn't drop the lantern as he scrambled back from the hole. "*Dios mío,* is that …"

Margot inched forward and peered into the hole to find a set of small human remains. The sight of it turned her stomach, but it also spurred her to action. She looked at Pedro. "Don't touch anything else. We need to call the police."

Margot dragged Pedro away by the arm back upstairs to the main floor of the church. His eyes had glazed over and he was silent. Shock did strange things to the human body. She ushered him into one of the last pews in the sanctuary. "Stay here. I'm going to call them."

"Who was it?" he finally mumbled.

"You're going to be okay," she said, not answering his question.

He shook his head and buried his face in his hands. Margot gave him a pat on the shoulder before retreating to her office. She knew she should dial 9-1-1, but instead she hit the Speed Dial *Number 3* on her contacts and waited as it rang.

"Is this a social call?" Sam commented after the third ring.

Officer Samantha Raymond was an up and coming officer on the Port Marie police force and she was also Margot's younger cousin. They'd worked together to solve Warren Nesbit's murder. She was the only person Margot trusted to solve the mystery sitting in the church basement. And unlike most of the other officers on the force, she was less likely to tell Margot to keep her nose out of things.

"Unfortunately, no. You need to get to the church now. We found something and you need to see it."

"Okay. I'll be there."

Margot said a silent prayer of thanks that her cousin didn't ask too many questions.

Sure, they'd butted heads the last time they'd worked together—then again Margot was the one who saw them as a partnership more than Sam—but Sam was a good investigator.

Satisfied that law enforcement was en route, Margot returned to the sanctuary and sat beside Pedro. She took one of his hands in hers and gave it a firm squeeze.

"You're going to be okay," she repeated.

"It was so small," he said, his voice croaking with emotion.

She tried not to think about what she'd witnessed even though it was already burned into her memory. Having a clear head would serve them both better when Sam arrived.

They fell into silence and Margot closed her eyes, focusing on her breathing. A sense of calm overtook her just as a hand tapped her shoulder. Margot jolted and opened her eyes. Sam stood before her.

"That was fast," Margot said, releasing Pedro's hand.

"You made it sound urgent."

Margot nodded and stood, heading toward the stairs to the basement.

Sam fell into step beside her. Jerking her chin toward Pedro, she asked, "What's up with him?"

"You'll see," Margot answered and started down the creaking steps.

For a split second, Margot expected what they'd found to have been a trick of light or their imagination, that when they stepped into the room the wall wouldn't be hiding anything at all.

"It's in here," Margot announced. She let Sam go ahead of her into the room.

Sam covered her mouth instantly. "What is that smell?"

Without the wall acting as a barrier the scent of decay filled the room. "It's coming from inside the wall."

Sam shuffled forward and used the lantern light to peer into the hole. She stepped back, just like Pedro had done. "That's a body."

"I think there might be another one," Margot said, taking shallow breaths.

Sam glanced at her over her shoulder. "Where?"

Margot gestured to the patch of older paint. "This area sounded hollow when I tapped on it."

Margot expected Sam to pick up the sledge hammer and take a swing at the wall. Instead, she reached for the radio clipped to her belt. "This is Officer Raymond, requesting a forensics team to the interfaith church. We've got at least one dead body."

"Copy," the dispatcher answered, their tone muffled by the crackle of the radio.

"Want to tell me how you found this?" Sam prompted.

Margot gestured toward the stairs. "Can we talk up there?"

Sam nodded and they retreated up the

flight of stairs. The air was less pungent and they both relaxed. Margot settled on the landing. "I was in the office working on Sunday's sermon when Pedro let me know about some water damage in the basement. He'd gone down to check the electrical panel and the boiler given all the storms, and there was an odd smell. We went down to check it out. There was definitely a smell and I noticed the paint looked different. I mean, the same color, but you could tell it had been painted over many different times."

"So, you decided to just start punching holes in it?" Sam asked with a mixture of amusement and annoyance.

"I thought it made sense to see if we could find the source of the smell so we'd know who to call to solve the problem. And, it worked. You are the right person to solve this particular problem," Margot answered with a shrug and sheepish grin.

"Why is it every time we see each other

these days, it's over a dead body?" Sam smiled.

Margot laughed. "Just luck, I suppose."

Heavy footfalls announced the forensic team's arrival. Two jumpsuit-clad men with cases approached. Margot didn't recognize them, but the town had more than two forensic technicians.

"There's a body down in the basement. Well, a skeleton. Reverend Quade thinks there may be a second body, too," Sam explained.

"I can show you," Margot offered before Sam could stop her. She led them down the stairs and pointed out the spot that had sounded hollow.

"We'll take it from here," one of the technicians said and set about examining the first set of remains.

Sam grabbed Margot by the arm and led her back upstairs to the sanctuary. Pedro still sat in the pew with his head bowed.

"He's the one who unearthed the remains," Margot said in a hushed tone.

"I'll get someone to come take his statement when he's ready. I'll need you to do the same," Sam responded.

"I'm happy to do it now to get it over with."

"We'll need to go over to the precinct to type it up. I'd rather wait until the guys downstairs do their thing and we know what we're dealing with."

They settled a few pews away from Pedro. Margot couldn't remember anyone talking about maintenance work in the basement since she'd been at the church.

"What's on your mind?" Sam prodded.

"I was trying to remember if there was ever talk of the basement being redone or having work done on it in the entire time I've been here. I can't think of any."

"Just because they didn't talk about it doesn't mean it wasn't done. We were kids.

How much did we pay attention during those annual meetings when they talked about the budget?"

Sam had a point. Margot and Sam had spent most of those meetings in the back of the sanctuary playing tic-tac-toe on that Sunday's order of service pamphlets.

Maybe she could go back through old work orders for clues. Or she could go to the one person who would know. "You know, there's someone who could tell us if there was anything going on that wasn't talked about in the wider congregation," Margot said.

"I'm listening."

"Conrad Baptiste, the previous custodian."

Conrad had resigned a few years back, when Reverend Hawley retired. According to her predecessor, Conrad's resignation letter cited back pain and advanced age as the primary reasons he could no longer care for the church. At least, that's what Reverend Hawley told her when it came time to fill the position.

"I'm not sure he'd be willing to talk to us," Sam answered.

"Why not? I always thought he was a nice guy."

"You missed a lot while you were away. After he left, he stopped coming to church. Or going out at all. He embraced the label of shut-in."

"So, he's eccentric."

"People like their privacy, which is fine. But it didn't go unnoticed that he stepped out of the public eye. If you think he'll talk, I can send a patrol car by his place."

If Conrad had withdrawn from society, Margot suspected Reverend Hawley put him on the weekly meals list from the church. She couldn't imagine Reverend Hawley not making certain Conrad was taken care of given his length of service to the church community. Before she could make the suggestion to check the list, the two technicians trudged up from the basement.

"You were right, Rev. There was a second body," one of them said.

I didn't want to be right. Something Pedro mentioned came back to her.

"The first set of remains looked small," she said. *Childlike,* she thought, but she didn't want to say it out loud.

"Given the size, both appear to be the remains of children," the tech confirmed. "From the anatomy we can gather, they were male. Given the growth markers, I think they were pre-pubescent or early teenagers. We'll know more once we can get them back to the lab and run more comprehensive tests."

"I'd better call this in to the precinct," Sam said and stood up.

"I need to check something before I join you to give my statement," Margot said.

"Okay," Sam said, "but don't take too long."

She would also need to notify members that the church couldn't be used for any services until the police released the crime scene in the basement.

"I'll put something up on the website and let the other worship leaders know we've discovered some structural issues after the storms," Margot said. "Until we can get them resolved, services are suspended."

"Good idea." Sam followed the techs out of the sanctuary, leaving Margot and Pedro alone.

"I know this is overwhelming, but you're going to need to give a statement to the police about what you found. I'll go with you," Margot whispered.

"Okay."

Pedro didn't look ready to move under his own power, so Margot looped an arm around his shoulders to help guide him to his feet.

"We just need to make a quick stop in my office," she told him. She would give her statement to Sam, but she needed to check those meal recipient logs first.

3

The meal delivery records weren't hard to find and as Margot had suspected, Conrad had been a recipient for a few years. The next scheduled delivery wasn't until tomorrow, but Margot was sure bringing the meal to him a day early wouldn't be a problem. Besides, she could twist Reverend Hawley's arm to accompany her. He wouldn't mind paying a visit to an old friend.

In short order, additional officers arrived at the church and cordoned off the basement stairs with crime scene tape. Margot hated that the church was unusable until the police concluded their investigation, but she understood the necessity.

Armed with the information she needed to pay Conrad a visit, Margot accompanied Pedro the precinct. Officer Weiss manned the dispatch desk just as he had months ago during the Nesbit investigation. He looked up and gave them a knowing nod.

"Officer Raymond is waiting for you both in the bull pen." He gestured to a doorway to their left.

Sam sat at one of the desks in the center of the room. She looked up from the computer screen in front of her and waved them over. Margot ushered Pedro forward. The shock of what he'd witnessed was wearing off, but he looked exhausted. The sooner he could give his statement and get some rest, the better. Margot made a mental note to call his older sister, Belinda, so he wouldn't be alone later.

"You should take Pedro's statement first. He needs to get home and get some rest," Margot said, plunking the custodian down in the seat next to Sam's desk.

"Sure. Why don't you go over to Officer Katz and she'll take your statement," Sam answered, addressing Pedro directly.

Pedro looked to Margot, wordlessly seeking her guidance. She gave his shoulder a firm squeeze. "I'll be over here if you need me."

He accepted her vote of confidence and marched three desks over, sitting down beside Officer Katz. Margot took his place beside Sam's desk.

"So, what do I have to do?" Margot knew from her last encounter with the law what giving a statement entailed. But Sam drummed on the edge of the desk with her fingers, and

Margot picked up on her nerves. In the back of her mind, Margot hoped explaining police procedure to a civilian would give her cousin a chance to do something familiar.

"I already put together what you told me," Sam said with a small smile. "You'll just need to read it over, make any necessary changes, then sign and date it like you did last time."

"Right. Um … You look nervous."

Sam raked her fingers through her auburn locks. "Not nervous, exactly. The lab guys have some high-tech equipment that dated the remains. The one in the new section of wall is about a decade old and older set was twenty."

Margot stared at Sam, dumbfounded. *How could two children's remains have been left unnoticed for so long?* Someone out there knew who these children were and how they got there. "That's unbelievable."

Sam leaned in closer, casting her gaze about to make sure no one paid them too much attention. "I shouldn't be telling you this, but it looked like there were some score marks on the bones, probably from a knife. It isn't confirmed yet but I'm guessing someone stabbed them."

Margot wished Sam hadn't filled her in on those details. As gruesome as they were, they only piqued her curiosity. For the second time, Sam had divulged sensitive case information to a civilian. Margot's brow furrowed. "No, you shouldn't have told me that. That's part of an active police investigation."

Sam worried her lower lip. "I know. Look, you were helpful with the Warren Nesbit case and this one is basically in your house. I know you well enough to realize you aren't going to let this go. You'll dig into it whether I want you to or not. Just, anything you find, run by me before you do anything. Promise me."

"Isn't that against the law? Won't anything I find be inadmissible?"

"You let me worry about the legalities. Just promise me that with anything you come across, you fill me in."

Margot mulled over her response. Sam was right in one respect: Margot had no intention of letting this drop. She couldn't simply walk away, especially after she was involved in the discovery of the remains. Too many unanswered questions remained. *Who were the children? Had they been reported missing?* Did she know either of them? She would have been old enough to remember the disappearance of a child twenty years ago. The death of a local child a decade ago would be fresher. Nothing came to mind in that moment though.

"Okay," she finally said. "I promise to call you if I find anything. But I can't imagine what I'd find."

"Be straight with me, Margot. Where are you planning to go next?"

Margot's cheeks burned a little with embarrassment. Her cousin was better at her job than she her credit for. "I was going to see Reverend Hawley to ask him if he remembers anything about work being done on the basement during his time at the church. If he does, I'll pass it on to you."

"Okay. Good. Margot, until we have more information, you can't mention what you found in the basement."

"You have my word."

Sam glanced over at Pedro. "We'll make sure someone gets Pedro home after he finishes his statement and make sure he understands he needs to keep quiet, too."

"Call his sister. He shouldn't be alone right now."

Sam gave her a sad smile. "Will do."

Margot waited while Sam printed out the statement she'd put together. Margot read the contents carefully, impressed with her cousin's recall of their conversation. She signed her name at the bottom and dated it.

Now, it was time to pay her mentor a visit.

"I hope you can figure out who those children are," Margot said and gave Sam a sympathetic look.

"Thanks."

Pedro was still deep in conversation with Officer Katz as Margot pulled her cell phone out of her jacket pocket and dialed Reverend Hawley's number.

Reverend Hawley answered on the second ring. "Margot, this is unexpected. How are you?"

"I'm okay. I was hoping you had time for a little visit?"

"For my favorite pupil, you know I do. Why don't you come by the house? I'll put some coffee on."

"I'll be right over."

Margot ended the call and headed for her car, formulating a version of the truth she could share with him that wouldn't get her in trouble.

"Come in, come in." Reverend Hawley ushered her inside before she could even ring the doorbell.

"Retirement suits you," she commented as she took off her shoes at the front door and hung her coat on a peg in the foyer.

"I'm enjoying a little quiet reflection these days. Remind me, do you take milk and sugar in your coffee?"

"You've got a good memory," she said with a smirk. That boded well.

She followed him into the living room and settled onto the couch. Even though it was warmer outside than it had been in weeks, a cozy fire burned in the hearth. Reverend Hawley returned to the room carrying two mugs of coffee. Margot accepted hers with both hands and inhaled the rich aroma.

He sat in an overstuffed armchair across from her. She took a few sips of her drink to prepare herself for the conversation.

"Something is weighing on you, Margot. I can see it on your face. What's wrong?"

She set her cup down on a coaster. "You were always good at reading people. I did actually have something I needed to ask you."

"I'm all ears."

She needed to be careful how much she revealed. He'd likely seen the notice she'd put up about services being cancelled for the foreseeable future. "We found some structural issues in the basement today at the church. I didn't find any invoices about work being done. Do you remember if there had been any problems before?"

Reverend Hawley rubbed his chin, his gaze trained on the dancing flames in the hearth. "I can check the records I have here but I don't remember any work being done down there. What sort of issues did they find?"

"Uh, there were mismatched paint layers on one of the walls." It was the truth. He didn't need to know about the entombed bodies.

"To be honest, I didn't go down there much. You know who you should speak with? Conrad Baptiste."

Margot hid a knowing smile behind the rim of her coffee mug. "Does he still live on the edge of town?"

"As far as I know. Though I haven't heard from him in a few months. He retired because of his back. I visited him for a while after that and convinced him to get on the meal delivery program."

"I'll have to see if I can get ahold of him, then."

"Do you have any idea how long it will take to get the issues cleared up? I can help you make other arrangements for services if you'd like."

"Oh, that's very kind of you, thank you. I appreciate the help. And no, we aren't sure yet how long we'll be out of commission. We still need to have someone come out and tell us what we're really dealing with." She hated lying to her mentor.

"Whatever I can do to help, please let me know. I may not be leading services there anymore, but I still consider that church my home."

"And we are always glad to see you and accept your generosity." She paused to collect her thoughts. "If you wouldn't mind, would you come with me to talk to Conrad? He doesn't really know me and I'm sure he'd be happy to see a familiar face."

"Of course. We can go now if you'd like."

"Oh, you know what, why don't we go over tomorrow morning? He's scheduled to have a meal delivered. We can take it over together."

"Sounds perfect. I'll meet you there."

"I'll see you tomorrow morning, then." Margot downed the rest of her coffee. "Thanks again for chatting with me."

"Anytime."

Margot showed herself out. Conrad Baptiste held the answers after all. Every sign pointed to him. *Please let him remember something.* She would let Sam know they were going over to talk to him in the morning. Assuming officers hadn't already made contact with him today. She had the keys in the ignition when her phone rang, displaying Sam's cell phone number.

"I was just about to call you," she answered.

"Can you come back to the precinct?" Sam's voice was hushed and strained.

"What's wrong?"

"Can you tell me why?" A sense of dread gnawed at her stomach.

"I'll explain when you get here."

The abruptness of the call and the evasiveness Sam exhibited set Margot on edge. Whatever Sam needed to share couldn't be good.

4

Sam waited outside the precinct when Margot pulled into the parking lot. She climbed into the passenger seat before Margot could turn off the engine.

Margot turned sideways to face her. "You're worrying me, Sam. What's going on?"

"You have an in with Conrad Baptiste, right?"

"I wouldn't call Reverend Hawley an 'in', he's more like an old friend. He suggested

Conrad as the best person to talk to if you're looking for a lead."

Sam pinched the bridge of her nose. "I ran his name through the system just to verify his address and something came up. He had a son named Thomas who ran away about twenty years ago."

Margot frowned. "I don't see how that's relevant."

"You know what I'm getting at," Sam argued.

"Spell it out for me." Her palms grew slick with sweat as her mind filled in pieces like a Mad Lib that she didn't want to believe to be true.

Sam turned in the seat so she faced Margot. "I don't think he went missing."

"That's a leap, Sam. Don't jump to conclusions just because it would make your job easier."

"I'm not jumping to conclusions. I'm

telling you it seems suspicious that he's at the heart of this thing."

Margot shook her head. "I'll admit that it is tragic that his child went missing around the time the first boy died. That is heartbreaking. But right now, it's just a tragic coincidence."

Even as the words left her mouth, Margot doubted their validity.

"I need to talk to him. Are you still planning to see him?" Sam asked.

"We're not going until tomorrow. Reverend Hawley and I are bringing him his weekly meal."

"I'll meet you over there, then."

Margot wanted to argue with her and insist that she didn't need a police chaperone. She also knew it was futile to object.

"Of course." After a moment of silence, Margot asked, "Do you know when you'll be able to release the crime scene in the basement? I understand you need to do your job, but it would be good to set expectations with the congregation. Reverend Hawley agreed to set up alternate arrangements, but that will only work for so long."

"We'll release it when we're satisfied that we've collected everything we can get out of it."

That was not the answer Margot had hoped for. "Okay. Try to keep me in the loop on that so I know what's happening with the church."

"Will do. I'll see you tomorrow," Sam answered and climbed out of the car.

Margot sat in the parking lot for a solid five minutes, contemplating her next move. She settled on going home to collect her thoughts in a place where she felt comfortable.

The trip from the precinct to her one-bedroom apartment a half mile from the church took no time at all. She entered the small space and took stock of her sparse furnishings.

If being overseas had taught her anything, it was that possessions didn't matter in the end. They only weighed a person down. Margot furnished the place with mementos from her time abroad as well as the family and friends she had reconnected with upon her return, but nothing over the top. Some habits were hard to break, including the need for order. She was up at seven o'clock every day and her bed was made even if she didn't leave the house.

At present, she needed to quiet the thoughts racing in her head. Sam's disclosure about Conrad's son stuck with her. She'd dismissed Sam's suspicions, but what if Sam was right?

The investigation would eventually identify the remains, but Margot's curiosity overwhelmed her. She couldn't wait that long. While she couldn't remember anything specific about the missing boy from her childhood, the local news likely had something. Small towns were notorious for reporting the big scandals in their community, and Port Marie was no different.

With her laptop in hand, Margot curled up beneath a handmade blanket from her mother and found the town's newspaper archives on the public library website. For a small town, Port Marie was surprisingly modern. All of the news articles had been digitized about a decade ago. She typed *Conrad Baptiste* into the search bar and waited for the results to load.

Only one article popped up.

Local Church Custodian's Son Vanishes

By: Veronica Morris, Staff Writer

Tragedy has befallen Port Marie as fourteen-year-old Thomas Baptiste, son of Conrad Baptiste and Maureen Prescott, vanished without a trace. According to court records, Mr. Baptiste and Ms. Prescott separated some time ago and Thomas alternated time with his parents. Ms. Prescott resides in a nearby town just over the Vermont border. Speculation abounds whether his parents' strained relationship led the young man to run away from home.

On the evening of March 17th, Ms. Prescott reported to police that her son never returned to her home as had been arranged after a visit with his father. Mr. Baptiste informed authorities he had placed his son on the bus back to his mother's residence and never saw his son again.

At this time, the police do not believe either parent to be involved in Thomas' disappearance. Anyone with any information about the young man's whereabouts are urged to contact the Chief of Police.

The article listed the phone number for the precinct—it hadn't changed in twenty years—and little else. No follow-up story existed on whether Thomas was ever located. The article dislodged a memory from her sophomore year of high school.

"I remember now," she murmured to the empty apartment.

Thomas' disappearance had been the talk of the town for a couple weeks until the case went cold. The candle light vigil held at town hall was the first time Margot had really prayed for something. She prayed for his safe return, but God hadn't heard her prayer back then. He'd also failed to answer when her best friend, Penelope and her sister Olivia had gone missing a year later. Maybe now she would get some answers to one of the two mysteries that had marred her teenage years.

She studied the article again. It had a small black and white photo of Thomas off to the side. It was grainy from being scanned and uploaded, but she could picture him from school; passing him in the hallways. They hadn't shared any classes together, but he'd been well-liked from what she remembered. Sam had been in his class. Maybe she remembered more, too. *What happened to you?*

If Sam's hunch was right and Thomas' remains had been located in the basement, at least Conrad might have an answer. Margot only hoped he would be willing to help the investigation.

5

Morning dawned and Margot rose before the sun. She'd been unable to get the image of Thomas' missing person's photo or the remains out of her thoughts. Despite all she'd witnessed overseas, the loss of children cut deep, especially when they'd been entombed in a place that was meant to bring peace and comfort.

She poured her coffee into a travel mug, prepared to down it on the trip over to Conrad Baptiste's house, when a knock at the door caught her off guard. Even though the meal was dinner, deliveries were made in the mornings by volunteers. He'd be expecting it so they wouldn't catch him off guard.

Setting the mug aside, she answered it to find Sam waiting on the other side of the threshold. Her cousin sported dark circles under her eyes and she shifted her weight from foot to foot.

"What are you doing here?" Lack of sleep clouded her own thoughts.

"Did you forget I'm coming with you on your meal delivery to Conrad Baptiste?"

Margot blinked, their prior conversation coming back to her. "Right. I assumed you'd meant to meet me there."

"Guess I'm a little eager to speak with Conrad."

"I did some light reading last night," Margot admitted before grabbing her mug and following Sam downstairs to a waiting patrol car.

"Please tell me it wasn't anything you shouldn't have access to."

"Not unless archived news articles are suddenly off limits. There was just one article about Thomas' disappearance from the paper, but no follow up articles. After they reported he went missing, nothing else was ever discovered." Margot set her coffee in the center console. "I remember him now. He was in your year at school."

Sam started the engine. "I know. It came back to me when I pulled the file and recognized his picture."

"Was there any good news in the file?" Maybe he'd been found and it just hadn't made the news.

"No. The case went cold. The officers back then talked to both parents. There was confirmation of a bus ticket purchased but witness' statements conflicted on whether anyone saw Thomas actually get on the bus.

Ultimately, they couldn't ever find anything conclusive."

"So, we're going to be dredging up bad memories for this man who hasn't had closure in twenty years." Margot frowned.

"Relax. I'm not going to push him too hard if that's what you're worried about. I just want to know what he knows about the basement."

They arrived at Conrad's split-level home ten minutes later. The outside had seen better days. Water stained the siding and loose shingles dangled on the roof. With his bad back and the heartbreak of losing a child, it wasn't unreasonable to let outward appearances go.

Reverend Hawley's truck was parked down by the mailbox. He climbed out, a container in one hand, as he waved to Sam and Margot.

"I didn't realize this required a police escort," he commented with a soft chuckle.

Margot wasn't sure how to respond. She'd been careful to keep the true nature of situation at the church quiet, like Sam asked.

"We were having breakfast and I was heading this way so I offered to give Margot a lift," Sam lied far more effortlessly than Margot was comfortable with.

"Oh, that was thoughtful of you," he said with an amiable grin. "If you're here, you might as well stay. I'm sure Conrad will be happy for the extra company."

The three of them marched up the cracked front steps and Reverend Hawley rang the bell. Margot could hear the tone of the doorbell echoing inside the house. She resisted the urge to peek into the bay window. It didn't stop Sam from taking a peek though.

"Maybe he's not awake yet," she said.

It was a reasonable assumption for a man of his age. Besides, the car that had been parked in front of the garage didn't look like it had run in quite a while.

"He's always been an early riser. I thought I got up early but he always beat me to the church in the mornings," Reverend Hawley said and opened the screen door, thumping his fist on the wood a couple of times.

That seemed to rouse the occupant, because the door opened about a minute later and Conrad Baptiste stared at the three of them crowded upon his front step.

"Reverend Hawley," he said, "what are you doing here?" Pale blue eyes peered at them from sunken sockets. His grey hair covered his scalp in thin wisps and his skin was extremely pale, as if he hadn't seen the sun in years.

He held up the container of food. "It's been a while since I paid you a visit and I knew it was delivery day. I wanted to see how you're doing."

Conrad nodded, regarding Margot and Sam with more suspicion. "And you ladies?"

Margot extended her hand. "Margot Quade, sir. I've taken over Reverend Hawley's position as minister at the church. And this is Officer Samantha Raymond."

Conrad shook her hand. She noted his veins and the weakness of his grasp. He was frail.

He said, "Thanks for the food but now's not really a good time for a visit. I haven't been feeling well."

"We won't stay long. We were just hoping you might remember some things about church renovations," Margot said.

Conrad's brow furrowed as he focused on Margot's face. "I suppose you can come in for a minute."

She smiled. "Thank you so much."

Margot, Sam, and Reverend Hawley moved into the front hall and followed Conrad into a sparse living room. It was furnished with a couple of wicker chairs and a sofa that had seen better days. Margot looked around and was surprised by what she saw. The mantle was lined with photos of his son at varying ages leading up to when he went missing. If she had to choose a word for it, she would have called it a shrine.

"I don't remember any renovations," Conrad said, reclaiming Margot's attention.

"You know, I think you're right," Reverend Hawley said, taking a seat on the couch.

Margot sat beside him. Sam leaned on the arm of the sofa and tracked Conrad's every movement. Now that they were inside, Conrad seemed nervous and fidgety. Margot cleared her throat.

"It might not have been anything official," Margot said. "We just noticed some different paint patches in the basement. Do you remember if there was ever any reason that sections would need to be painted over? Maybe water damage or anything like that?"

Conrad stroked his chin and his eyes went unfocused. At least he was trying to remember. "Not that I recall. But I worked at the church for a long time. I can't remember everything I did there."

"We understand that," Reverend Hawley said, starting to stand. "Don't worry too much. I'm sure everything will be fine."

"While we're here, I was hoping to ask you a couple of questions about your son, Thomas," Sam interjected.

Reverend Hawley whipped his head around to look at Sam with a surprised expression. Margot was beginning to regret not filling her mentor in on the situation. Objectively she understood she couldn't share the details of an ongoing police matter with him, but it would have been better if he hadn't betrayed his surprise at the sudden change in questions.

Conrad mirrored Sam's suspicious expression. "Why do you want to know about Thomas?"

"I'm relatively new to the department, but I was looking through some cold cases," Sam said. "When Margot mentioned you had been the custodian at the church, it made me remember that your son was one of those cases I had looked at. I was in the same grade as him. I think we had a few classes together. Anyway, I'm interested in seeing if I could find out anything new about the case."

Margot knew most of her cousin's statement wasn't true, and she had to admit she was impressed with how easily Sam fed the older man the lie. Telling falsehoods was a sin according to the Bible, and yet Margot had to constantly remind herself how lying had become a part of human society and their culture. Her chest tightened for a moment as she reminded herself that she was engaging in the behavior, too.

"I don't know what else I could tell you besides what I told the police back then. I put Thomas on that bus back to his mom and he never made it there," Conrad answered in a flat, emotionless tone.

"I know this is hard to talk about, but did you get the sense that Thomas wanted to run away before then?" Sam pressed.

"He wasn't happy his mother and I split up. But honestly, what kid is happy about a divorce?" His voice took on a tinge of bitterness at the mention of his ex-wife.

"Right, I'm sure it was hard on everyone," Sam said in a compassionate voice. "It's a big change. But he never mentioned wanting to run away? Did you reach out to any of his friends in the area?"

"No, he never said he wanted to run away."

Conrad looked over his shoulder, as if checking to make sure they weren't being overheard. The fidgeting that Margot had noticed when they first sat down returned. "I have things to do. I'm sorry, but I'm going to have to ask you to leave."

"It was good to see you, Conrad," Reverend Hawley said and passed him the meal container.

Margot offered her hand and he shook it swiftly before disappearing into the kitchen. She followed after him. "Would you mind if I used your bathroom before we leave?"

"It's back down the hall on the right."

"Thank you. And again, we really appreciate your time this morning."

He nodded. "Sorry I couldn't be more helpful."

She retraced her steps and saw that Sam and Reverend Hawley were waiting at the front door. "I'll be there in just a minute. I need to use the bathroom."

She followed the front hall around to the left and spotted a door that was partially open. Curiosity really was her biggest flaw and the one thing she found she couldn't turn off or ignore. It wouldn't hurt to just take a quick look. She nudged the door open more with her foot and peered in. It appeared to be Thomas' room, given the decorations: 80s action movie posters clung to the walls, some had the corners peeling up. A desk sat in one corner with small military figurines lined up in a neat formation. Laundry remained on the floor and even the bed was messy. *Had Conrad left the room untouched in the hopes it would one day be in use again?* It was certainly a typical trait of a parent who'd lost a child. Still the bedclothes looked fresh, not marred by years of sun damage and age. Whoever had slept in the bed had done so recently.

She closed the door again and stepped across the hall into the bathroom. As she washed her hands minutes later, she couldn't shake the feeling that was beginning to settle over her—the feeling that maybe Conrad knew more than he was letting on about his son's disappearance.

She returned to the front of the house. "Goodbye, Mr. Baptiste," she called, receiving no answer.

By the time she rejoined Sam in the car, Reverend Hawley's truck was gone.

"Everything okay?" Sam asked as she put the car in reverse and backed out of the driveway.

Margot considered keeping what she'd seen from Sam, but knew it wouldn't do any good. If Sam found out another way later on, it would only fill their relationship with distrust. "I noticed something when I was going to the bathroom."

"That he leaves the seat up?" Sam offered with a smirk.

"The room he kept for Thomas. I'm pretty sure someone is sleeping in there now. There were clothes on the floor and the bed was unmade. At first I guessed that he kept the room just like his son had left it, but the bedsheets looked new. And the clothes don't look like what a teenage boy would have worn twenty years ago."

"What are you saying?" Sam pressed.

"I don't know. I'm just telling you what I saw. I don't think Conrad is living alone. Maybe Thomas came home and he just never told anyone?" She brightened at the idea.

"Maybe."

From the center console, Sam's phone beeped with an incoming call. She scooped it up and pressed it to her ear. "Officer Raymond."

The crackle of another voice came through over the line, but it was too muffled for Margot to pick out individual words. The fact that Sam's expression went from neutral to unhappy told her that it wasn't good news.

"I understand," Sam said. "Thank you."

As soon as Sam ended the call, Margot asked, "What's happened?"

"They managed to identify the more recent body. It belonged to another missing person's case. Henry Dalton. He went missing from Port Marie ten years ago."

6

Margot knew the Dalton family. They had been members of the church for as long as she'd been there and were at service every week, sitting in the same pew. How had she missed that they, too, had a child go missing? She wanted to offer them support when Sam broke the news.

"Look, I know you want to be there, but we need to do this by the book as much as possible," Sam said, as if reading Margot's mind.

"How did I not know he'd gone missing?"

"It happened after you had already left for seminary. I remember it pretty well though. He was in his front yard one afternoon and then he just vanished. People searched for days but never found anything. The police didn't have any leads either. Just like with Thomas."

Margot hoped Sam would at least let her provide pastoral counseling to her congregants. "Can you tell them that I'm here if they need to talk?"

"I'll pass it on."

"You can drop me back at home," Margot said, intent on learning all she could about Henry's abduction.

Ten minutes later, Margot sat with her laptop on her knees, digging through the newspaper archives to find anything on Henry's disappearance. She found that there was only one article that had been uploaded. *Just like Thomas.* This one was dated March

17th, exactly like the one from Thomas' disappearance ten years' earlier.

Another Local Boy Vanishes, Leaving Port Marie Rocked

By: Veronica Morris-Sawyer, Staff Writer

Ten years to the day, another member of the Port Marie community has vanished without a trace. Eleven-year-old Henry Dalton was last seen playing in his front yard by his parents and neighbors. He was discovered missing when his mother went to call him in for dinner. Search parties, including many volunteers from the local church, have been dispatched, but so far, they have not located Henry.

People are quick to point out the similarity to Thomas Baptiste's disappearance. For those who may not remember, Thomas Baptiste disappeared after boarding a bus headed out of town. His case remains open and unsolved. Police are asking anyone with any information to reach out to the tip line that has been set up.

As we come together to support the Daltons, speculation abounds. Are the two cases connected? And if they are, what possible motive exists to link these boys?

The fact that Veronica was the same writer who covered the first story struck Margot as more than mere coincidence. What connection did she have to the missing boys? Was it simply a case of luck of the draw that set Veronica on the path to reporting on the disappearances? Or was there something more hidden within her words?

Like with Thomas' article, this one came with a school photo of the missing boy. The original had likely been printed in black and white, but when the records were digitized, the photo had been updated. Margot studied Henry's face for a long time. She tried to place him in her mind, but any connection she may have had remained just out of reach.

An incoming call disrupted her focus and she set aside the computer. "Hello, this is Margot," she answered.

"Reverend Quade, this is Roy Dalton," a high tenor voice said on the other end of the line.

"Officer Raymond said she would be speaking with you," Margot replied.

"She said we could come to you if we needed … support."

"Of course." She closed her laptop. "I can come over right now."

"Thank you."

Margot could hear how close Mr. Dalton was to breaking down, and her heart ached for his loss. "I'll see you soon."

SHE ARRIVED at the Dalton home and paused in the driveway. It had been a decade, but she could still see young Henry playing in the yard. *How had no one seen who took him? Did he know his abductor? Had he gone willingly?* Margot shook the images and litany of questions from her mind focusing her attention on being the steady rock this family needed her to be.

Margot knocked on the front door and waited. She could hear footsteps from within the house and was soon met by Roy Dalton. He had bags under his eyes and his cheeks were pale. His wife, Christina, appeared at his side, and Margot noted she'd been crying.

"Thanks for coming so quickly," Roy said.

"I am so sorry for your loss," Margot said.

"Please, come in. Don't mind the mess," Christina mumbled.

Margot followed them into the house and let the grieving couple lead her to the den. The heat from baseboard heaters filled the room with stuffy hot air, but she wouldn't complain. She took a seat on the couch and waited for them to join her.

"Would you like something to drink? Tea or coffee?" Christina was clinging to the formality of having a house guest.

"Tea would be great. Thank you."

Christina nodded, mostly to herself, and disappeared toward the kitchen. Roy sat across from Margot and wrung his hands. "We'd always hoped that Henry just took off and he'd come home one day."

"I'm so sorry that this was the news the police had to bring you."

"They said that he probably died not long after he disappeared." Tears slid down Roy's cheeks unbidden.

"I'm here for whatever you need. I'd be happy to hold a memorial for Henry, to honor his life."

"Thank you. I'm not sure if we're going to be able to bury our son. Officer Raymond said they can't release his … remains until they figure out who killed him."

"That's understandable. I'm sure the police are doing everything they can to find out what happened to Henry," Margot said.

Christina returned with a mug of tea. Her hands shook as she passed it over. Through a sob, she said, "They said they found him at the church."

Margot took a sip of tea to formulate her response. If the police had divulged the whereabouts of Henry's body, then it couldn't hurt to admit she knew that. "I know. I was there when he was discovered."

That piece of information had the opposite effect she'd hoped. Christina collapsed against her husband, sobbing more vigorously. Her whole body shook as Roy wrapped his arms around his wife. "How could he have been there this whole time and no one noticed?"

"I wish I had more answers for you," Margot replied.

"Why would God take our boy from us like this? And leave us wondering for so long?" Christina sniffled, trying to regain her composure.

Margot was at a loss. The God she believed in was benevolent and looked after his children. He wouldn't have allowed a child to suffer how it appeared Henry had. But, she knew that telling these people God didn't have a hand in their son's death wasn't the right answer.

"It is going to take time to make sense out of all of this."

She stood, needing to expend some nervous energy. She moved to the mantle which housed photos of Henry, much like Conrad Baptiste's mantle had displayed photos of Thomas. As she picked up a smiling picture of a happy child, she realized the connection her mind had tried to make: Henry bore a striking resemblance to Thomas Baptiste. Perhaps whoever took Thomas had seen those similarities, too.

What if there were others?

She knew what she needed to do. She had a date with the newspaper archives, yet again.

7

Thomas and Henry's abductions seemed less coincidental the more Margot considered the facts. Both had gone missing at the same time of year and were roughly the same age. Whoever took them had a "type," and as much as she wished they were the only ones, someone capable of such violence wasn't likely to stop unless they had been caught. They were quickly approaching the anniversary date and Margot couldn't shake the feeling that yet another boy was about to go missing. Or that there were others who had disappeared after Henry.

After a few false starts, she found an article from five years ago, again from mid-March, penned by the same staff writer as the others.

Third Boy Taken on Anniversary of Tragic Abductions

By: Veronica Morris-Sawyer, Staff Writer

In what is becoming a disturbing pattern, a third boy has gone missing from his Port Marie home. Fifteen-year-old Dustin Grady disappeared on his way home from school on the anniversary of the disappearances of Henry Dalton and Thomas Baptiste. The two other missing boys would now be in their late teens and early twenties. Their cases remain unsolved.

Could this be the work of the same

predator? According to police records, Dustin was a troubled boy and had brushes with the law on several occasions for minor vandalism and loitering. Police are examining all angles, including the possibility that Dustin simply ran away. His family was not on hand to comment on a possible motive for Dustin to leave town. It could just be a coincidence, but as always, anyone with information should contact the police tip line.

Margot looked at Dustin's photo accompanying the article. He bore an undeniable resemblance to Thomas and Henry. She searched the archives for news of missing children before Thomas' disappearance, but found none.

So, this had started with Thomas. If the police positively identified the second set of remains as Thomas, then who was occupying the bedroom in Conrad's home? For a fleeting moment the possibility that Dustin had somehow survived his abduction crossed her mind. *Why would he be different though?* He'd had brushes with the law where the other boys had clean records, but that couldn't be enough of a difference to convince a killer to spare his life. If he had met the same fate as the other boys, where were his remains? She knew Sam wouldn't divulge such details to her, but she needed to share her theory. Margot dialed Sam's cell phone and waited.

"This isn't a good time. I've got the press hounding me about why the church is closed," Sam answered in one long breath.

"I know you're busy, I just needed to tell you something about the case."

"I'm listening."

"After you identified Henry's remains, I went back and looked through the newspaper archives. There was another boy who went missing five years ago."

"Dustin Grady," Sam interrupted in a hushed tone.

"Right. He and Henry both bear a resemblance to Thomas. I don't want to speak for whoever did this, but it seems they have a type."

"I'll have the techs go back to the church and see if there's a third body."

"I know you shouldn't be telling me, but did they identify the other set of remains?" Margot questioned tentatively. She held her breath as she waited for Sam's response.

"They're taking longer. Look, I appreciate you letting me know about the other missing boy and the resemblance. It helps."

"Just do whatever you can to bring these boys justice," Margot said.

"I need to go. This reporter isn't going to leave me alone unless I give her a comment."

"Let me guess. Veronica Morris-Sawyer," Margot said with a chuckle.

"She a friend of yours?"

"She's the one who wrote about all three of the missing boys." Margot wouldn't say she'd made a career out of reporting on these disappearances, but her name hadn't shown up on many other articles in the paper's archives. All of her articles lacked real emotion for the situation. They gave little information about the circumstances surrounding the abductions or the grief and fear felt by those left behind. Margot's stomach did an uncomfortable flop as she realized what was bothering her.

"Sam, what if she's involved?" The words came out before she could stop them.

"What makes you think that?"

"The way the articles were written, they lacked empathy. Maybe it's nothing, but her name doesn't appear on many other articles."

"I'll keep that in mind," Sam said. "Thanks for the heads up."

"Be safe."

Margot ended the call, but her uneasiness

remained. She would let Sam follow up on Veronica, of course. At the same time, she couldn't shake her curiosity about who was sharing Conrad's home, living in Thomas' bedroom. Just maybe a visit unaccompanied by the police would make the older man more willing to speak openly.

MARGOT PAID CLOSER attention to the geography as she made the short trip to Conrad's house. He lived just two streets over from the Daltons. She didn't know the Grady's address off-hand, but she guessed they weren't far either. She began building a narrative in her mind, one that didn't sit well with her at all. Conrad was in close proximity to all three missing boys. But, what motive would he have to hurt them, including his own child?

She arrived at the Baptiste property to

find an empty driveaway. Given her initial impression of Conrad's frailty, she didn't believe he'd gone out. Still, she trudged up to the front door and knocked and waited.

Nothing happened.

Margot tried knocking louder. "Mr. Baptiste, it's Reverend Margot Quade from the church. Please can we talk?"

Still nothing.

She turned to leave and spotted a patrol car pulled up to the edge of the driveway, blocking her exit. Margot approached the car as the driver rolled down the window.

"What are you doing here, Margot?" Sam asked.

"I thought maybe Conrad would be more willing to talk about what happened to his son if it was just me rather than a group," she admitted. She brushed a few strands of hair from her face. "How'd it go with Veronica?"

"I gave her a vague quote and she went away."

"Are you looking into what I mentioned?"

"I will, but there's more pressing news. The techs identified the other set of remains. They belong to Thomas, like I suspected. I was just coming to break the news to Conrad. I called his ex-wife and let her know. She's driving down in the morning."

"It doesn't look like he's home," Margot noted, gesturing to the empty driveway.

Before Sam could comment, a voice crackled over the dispatch radio. It was loud enough that Margot could hear it from where she stood. "All units be advised, we have a report of a missing child."

That isn't just a coincidence. Margot was sure of it now that she'd uncovered the pattern. She waited while Sam jotted down the details. Martin Fairbanks.

She knew Martin. He was in the youth choir and a member of the interfaith youth group. He was a kind boy with a big heart. Her heart hammered against her ribs as fingers of icy dread slid down her spine. He also bore a resemblance to the other missing boys. *I should have seen this coming.*

"I know the family," Margot said.

Sam gave her a stern look. "I told you that you can't be a part of this investigation officially."

"I'm not. I am a family friend and their pastor. You sent me to the Daltons as their pastor. How is this any different? They're going to be distraught," Margot replied, her voice strained. If the fear that gripped her was any indication, his parents must be terrified.

"Fine. But, you need to hang back if I tell you."

"Of course," Margot answered and retreated to her own car. She said a silent prayer that they would be able to rescue Martin.

8

Margot pulled in behind Sam's patrol car three streets over from Conrad's home. She hung back until Sam was out of her car and marching up the short front walk. Margot fell into step behind her cousin and waited as Sam rang the bell. The door opened immediately and Cynthia Fairbanks stood on the other side of the threshold, eyes red-rimmed from crying.

"Thank God you're here," she said when she saw Sam.

"Mrs. Fairbanks, may we come in?" Sam said.

"Please."

Cynthia led them into a living room that was well lived-in. A board game which looked to be mid-play sat on the table. Margot knew that Cynthia's husband, Bernard, worked odd hours.

"Is your husband home, Mrs. Fairbanks?" Sam asked.

"No. He's at work. I called him as soon as I realized Marty was missing."

"Okay," Sam said. "Let's sit down and you can tell me what happened."

Margot settled next to her cousin and listened as Cynthia explained the circumstances leading to her son's disappearance.

"He stayed home from school today because he wasn't feeling well." She pointed to the board game. "I think he just wanted to spend some time with me. He's not old enough to stay home by himself. He's only thirteen. He thinks he's old enough but ..." she trailed off, tears staining her cheeks.

"Can you tell me when you noticed something was wrong?" Sam pressed gently.

"It was an hour ago maybe. I'd told him to go lie down for a bit. I went to check on him, and he was gone."

Sam asked in a compassionate voice, "Has he ever mentioned wanting to run away? Or maybe he went and saw a friend?"

"No, Marty is a good boy. He wouldn't run away. And all of his friends are in school. Who would he be going to see?'

"Have you noticed anyone out of place hanging around the house lately?" Margot interjected, earning a glare from Sam.

"Out of place? I don't think so. Like who?"

Margot shrugged in an effort to hide her line of questioning. "Anyone you didn't recognize?"

"No. I don't think so."

"Can I see his room?" Sam asked, getting to her feet.

"Of course. It's this way."

Cynthia shuffled into the hall and led them to the last room on the left. It looked like a typical teenage boy's room with action movie posters. The drapes and bedspread were a matching combination of deep greens and blues. They reminded Margot of the ocean. The bed wasn't made, but it also didn't look to Margot's untrained eye like he'd been taken against his will.

"Were his shoes missing?" she asked.

"I'm sorry?" Cynthia rasped.

Sam seemed to pick up on Margot's line of thought. "It doesn't look like he was taken from his room. It's possible he left of his own accord. Or at least with someone he knew. Did you notice if his shoes were missing, too?"

"I didn't check."

They returned to the front of the house.

Sure enough, his shoes and coat were missing. It appeared that Martin had gone willingly.

"Does Martin have a cell phone?" Sam was reaching for her own as she spoke.

"What teenager doesn't? He practically lives on that thing. I didn't see it in his room earlier."

"We'll need you to come down to the precinct to give a statement. We're also going to need his cell phone number so we can try and track him."

"Anything you need. Please, just find my son."

Sam gave her a sympathetic look and headed out, leaving Margot and Cynthia to stand in the front hall. Cynthia wrapped her arms around her torso, warding off some unseen chill. "I heard that the church is closed due to structural issues."

"We're working to get it resolved as soon as possible. Reverend Hawley and I are coming up with alternative meeting places in the meantime."

"I heard that they found bodies in the basement." Cynthia's voice was a whisper.

Margot stiffened. There were only a few people who knew that piece of information. "Where'd you hear that?"

"I do yoga with Belinda Sanchez. She said her brother Pedro was mumbling something about it. Is it true? Did they find bodies? Oh my God, is my Marty one of them?"

"I can't say. You'd have to ask the police. I want you to know that I will be here for you and your husband. Anything you need. I'd be happy to help."

"Please, just promise me they're going to find my Marty alive."

Margot couldn't make that promise. Given the pattern that had been established with the other missing boys, the police had a small window of time in which to find him.

"The police are going to do everything they can."

Cynthia nodded mutely. Her eyes were beginning to glaze over. Margot gave her a firm squeeze on the arm. "Come on, I'll take you to the precinct."

The trip across town was silent and short. Cynthia stared blankly out the passenger window. Margot wasn't in a talkative mood, either. She was beginning to wonder if Conrad could have been behind it all. It was a horrible thing to think of a man who had given so much of his life and time to the church. It didn't make sense that he'd want to harm his son or anyone else. But he was conspicuously absent right when Martin went missing. And there was another suspect —where was Veronica Morris-Sawyer at the time of Martin's disappearance?

"You know, I read those articles in the paper all those years ago when those other boys went missing. They never found them,"

Cynthia said in a monotone voice as Margot escorted her to the bullpen and Sam's desk.

Margot pulled another chair over and sat beside Cynthia as Sam took her statement. Some twenty minutes later, Bernard Fairbanks burst into the bullpen, his hair disheveled and wild-eyed.

"Cynthia! What happened?" he boomed.

Cynthia took one look at her husband and broke down sobbing. Margot wrapped her in a tight embrace and made soft shushing noises, letting Sam deal with the frantic husband.

"Mr. Fairbanks, your son has been reported missing. Your wife contacted us as soon as she realized what had happened. If you wouldn't mind, I'd like to talk to you," Sam said, physically intercepting him before he could reach his wife.

"Missing? How?"

Sam didn't respond. She just ushered him out of the bullpen and into a private room.

Cynthia's sobs subsided and Margot lightened her embrace.

"He's going to blame me," she whimpered.

"No, he's not. He's just as scared as you are. When you're finished, why don't you come over and I can make you something to eat."

"That's so kind of you. Thank you."

It was the least Margot could do. Besides, Bernard would be busy for a while with the police. Margot escorted Cynthia back to the car and they rode in silence to Margot's apartment.

"It isn't much," Margot said as they walked in. She'd left it a bit more of a mess than usual, with her computer open on the couch. It still had the news articles open and she quickly closed it.

"Why don't you have a seat?" Margot said. "I'll make us some sandwiches."

It wasn't going to be anything fancy, but she wanted to give Cynthia sustenance.

Margot filled her tea kettle just in case as she set about fixing the food. If she knew anything about the people in her town, they were tea drinkers.

"You know about the other boys who went missing, don't you?" Cynthia said from the couch.

"I've read about them. Yes."

"They were never found. What if that happens with … my Marty?"

"You have to stay positive, Cynthia. You have to have faith that the police will find him before anything bad happens to him."

"You just never think it's going to happen to you. Bad things are what happen to other people. I know it sounds horrible and even un-Christian. But, it's like God is punishing us for something and we don't know what we've done."

"The God I believe in is kind and doesn't hurt his people. I believe you'll see your son again and I believe he's going to be okay."

"You were there when they found those bodies weren't you?" Cynthia asked "You know what's really going on."

Margot left the kitchen to join Cynthia in the living room area. "I was, but I can't talk about it. It's an active police investigation."

Cynthia wrung her hands together. "I feel so hopeless like I have no control over anything."

"I understand." Margot squeezed Cynthia's shoulder, wishing it was that easy to offer someone strength. "I can't imagine how scared you are right now, but you're not alone. You have this entire community behind you."

Cynthia nodded dully.

Margot hesitated. "Do you mind if I ask you something?"

"Okay."

"Do you know Veronica Morris-Sawyer? She's a reporter."

"Port Marie is small, but that name

doesn't ring a bell." Cynthia's brow furrowed and her lips pursed. "Wait, no, I think I've seen the name before. She's the one who wrote the articles about the missing boys. Do you think she'll want to talk to us?"

"It's possible." Margot admitted to herself that she had little idea what could motivate Veronica to take the boys, let alone harm them. If she'd wanted notoriety for her career, she hadn't succeeded. That left only one other possibility. "Did Martin know Conrad Baptiste?"

"The old custodian from the church?"

Margot nodded and waited for Cynthia's response.

"I don't think so. At least not personally. They probably crossed paths at the church when Marty was little. But Conrad hasn't worked there in years. Why are you asking about him?"

"No reason," Margot said, trying to cover her digging.

"No, there is a reason." Cynthia's voice was stronger, and her eyes flashed with anger. "Wait, is he involved?"

"I really didn't mean anything by the question." But the damage was already done, the suspicion sown.

Margot retreated to the kitchen in time to catch her phone skittering across the counter since it was on vibrate. Sam's cell phone number flashed across the screen.

"Hey. Has Bernard calmed down?" Margot asked in a hush.

"Yeah. Look, where did you take Cynthia?"

"Back to my place. I figured she could use something to eat and some company away from the house."

"We tracked Martin's phone," Sam said. "A uniform found it on the side of the road. Like someone tossed it out of a moving car."

Margot headed toward the front of the apartment, the safest distance from Cynthia and said, "Sam, I have a bad feeling about this. What if it's Conrad?"

"I thought you were on the Veronica bandwagon."

"The more I think about it, I can't come up with a motive for her that makes sense."

"What makes you think it's Conrad?" Sam asked. "The officers who investigated Thomas' disappearance cleared him all those years ago."

"Come on, Sam. Didn't his answers seem a little rehearsed to you this morning? Besides, all of the boys bore a resemblance to Thomas. They all went missing within a mile of Conrad's home, and seem to happen around the same time of year, too."

Sam let out a long breath. "You're not wrong. It fits. But why would he stop for such long periods of time?"

"I don't know. Maybe these dates mean something specific to him. Did Thomas' remains have stab marks too?" It was a gamble whether Sam would give her a straight answer.

"Yes," Sam said quietly. "It looked like it."

He wouldn't be the first man to develop some sort of ritual in killing. "Did they find a third body?"

"No. Just those two."

That didn't make any sense. Unless Dustin escaped before Conrad could kill him. *If he broke free, where has he been for the last five years?*

"Sam, you should go back to Conrad's house. Martin could be there. Or the church."

"I'll send teams to both right now."

Margot ended the call. Sam may be sending reinforcements, but Margot had no idea if they'd arrive in time. Besides, she was closer. She parceled up the sandwiches and tea before stepping back into Cynthia's line of sight. "Cynthia, I think I should take you home. Just in case Martin comes back on his own. You don't want him to come home to an empty house."

"You're right," Cynthia said, her voice hoarse.

Her shoulders sagged as Margot ushered her back to the car. Time to save a boy's life.

9

The sun set behind the houses and tree line of Port Marie as Margot returned to the church, her muscles tensing. She knew that Sam was only a phone call away if she really needed her. Margot wasn't defenseless, though. She may have been a chaplain in the Army, but she'd been through basic training and had the same combat skills as her fellow soldiers. She hoped those skills wouldn't be necessary.

The church sat dark against the fading daylight. She pulled into the back parking lot and spotted the rickety pick-up truck she'd first seen in Conrad's driveway that morning. Margot held her breath as she approached the back door to the church. It sat propped open with a rock.

The rear of the church housed the kitchen, the fellowship hall, and the children's chapel. None of those connected to the basement; the only basement access consisted of the entrance she and Pedro had used the day before when this whole ordeal began. With cautious steps, Margot made her way to the sanctuary, noting two sets of muddy footprints on the carpet leading to the narthex. One set of prints was distinctly child-sized. She reached for the phone in her pocket to alert Sam only to find it wasn't there. She closed her eyes and bit her lip, realizing she'd left it in the front seat of her car. There was no time to go back and get it though. Martin's life was in danger.

Margot hoped the carpeting would

muffle her approach and she did her best to keep silent on the hardwood floor of the narthex.

Light filtered up the stairs from the basement. Forensic equipment sat discarded in front of her so the light had to be from the camping lantern and single bulb fixture down below. She silently berated herself again for leaving the phone in her car. She knew she should call Sam for back up, but she needed to save Martin if she could.

***

HALFWAY DOWN THE STAIRS, Margot picked up on hushed voices coming from below her; still too far to pick out distinct speakers. She took another step toward them, but her foot landed on one of the creaky steps.

The conversation ceased immediately.

Margot took an exaggerated step down the last two stairs and pressed herself to the wall, out of sight of the doorway. Like the back door, this one sat partially open too. It gave her a semi-obstructed view into the room. She waited, hoping the voices would resume. They did.

"I still don't get why we're down here," Martin Fairbanks said, his voice crackling with puberty.

"I told you, it's a game," replied a voice—a voice that did not belong to Conrad Baptiste. The speaker sounded much younger, in fact. Not much older than Martin himself.

Dustin maybe?

Without considering the consequences, Margot stepped into the doorway. She found Martin on his knees in the middle of the room, his hands bound together in front of him. She couldn't see his ankles, but she assumed they were bound, too. The other occupant looked similar enough to Martin and the others that it had to be Dustin Grady.

He'd aged a lot in the five years he'd been missing.

"Who are you?" Dustin snapped, the knife in his hand glinting in the yellow light. She was able to make out flecks of blood on it. Some of it was old and rust-colored. Some looked far fresher.

"I'm Margot. I'm a friend. Can you tell me what's going on here?" she asked, looking directly at Martin.

"I don't know. This is kind of freaking me out," Martin answered.

"Don't talk to her." Dustin turned and brandished the knife at her. "You're ruining it. You need to leave."

"Dustin—that's your name, right? Dustin Grady?" Margot took a step into the room, keeping her hands where he could see them. She slowly began working her way forward in the hopes of placing herself in his path, in front of Martin.

"I said you need to leave!" Spittle flecked from Dustin's mouth as he shouted.

"You know that I can't do that. A lot of people have been worried about you. Your parents, your friends." She took another step so that she was now in line with Martin.

Dustin's eyes widened and his cheeks flushed. "This isn't how it's supposed to happen."

"Tell me how it is supposed to happen, Dustin," Margot urged, shuffling another step to the left.

"It has to be him." He gestured to the boy still sitting bound on the floor. "I have to do it. I promised I would."

"Who did you promise?"

"I told him I'd do it and he let me live."

"Conrad Baptiste?" She now stood directly in his line of attack. If he wanted his young victim, Dustin would have to go through her first.

Dustin let out a gargled laugh. "He told

me he had to do it because God wanted him to. Can you believe that? He said he was tested and he passed the test, but then God said he had to do it again and again."

"With Thomas and Henry and you?" she prompted.

She swore she heard sirens in the distance. Dustin didn't appear to hear them though. Dustin began pacing back and forth, the handle of the knife pressed against his temple. She just needed a little more time to disarm him.

"Did he tell you why he chose you and the others? And why they happened when they did?" Margot asked.

"It's when God told him he had to be tested again. It was important he pass the test every time. He said a man has to know the different parts of life."

His words didn't make any sense. "What test? Help me understand, Dustin."

"He told me the story of when God told

Abraham to sacrifice his son. He said he had to do that, too."

Margot let out a sigh. "Did he tell you how that story ended? Isaac was spared."

"That was me. I was the one he saved," Dustin said, jabbing a finger toward his chest. "He said I was special. He showed me how to pass the test. He said I have to do it now."

"I'm so sorry that happened to you, Dustin. I truly am. But you don't have to do what he says. You can be free from him. Let me help you."

"Free?" Dustin took a step forward and brandished the knife again.

She nodded. "Yes. You can come home to your family." She began taking small steps forward, still keeping her hands where he could see them. As long as he didn't perceive her as a physical threat, she could take him down.

"But, he took care of me."

"Dustin, he kidnapped you and he tried to kill you."

"You don't understand anything," Dustin wailed, lunging forward.

For a brief moment, Margot stood rooted to the spot, surprised by his sudden move. Then her training kicked in. She reached forward and grabbed his wrist, twisting his arm behind his back. He struggled against her, the knife stabbing at empty air. The more he moved, the closer they staggered towards Martin.

"You don't have to do this," Margot grunted. "Conrad is sick. He needs help, too. But we can't help him unless you put the knife down."

Dustin struggled, kicking wildly, but she managed to wrangle him to the ground. She squeezed his hand until he finally dropped the knife. It skittered across the cold basement floor.

He let out another laugh and this time he

just kept laughing. Tears sprang to his eyes as Margot held onto him.

"You can't help him," Dustin rasped.

Out of the corner of her eye, Margot spotted Martin scooting along the floor toward the discarded blade. Footsteps thundered down the stairs and Sam appeared, her weapon drawn. Margot held Dustin in a tight embrace, his arms pinned at his side.

"We're okay," Margot called over her shoulder, hoping Sam would lower her gun.

"He wants to kill me," Martin said on a hoarse tone, the knife clutched in both hands.

"He's not going to hurt you. Just put that down, Marty," Sam said, her tone soft.

Until now, Martin had kept a brave face. At the sound of Sam's soft voice, tears dampened Martin's cheeks and the knife slid from his fingers. Sam pulled him close and retrieved a utility knife from her gear, sliding the blade through the rope at his wrists and ankles.

"Next time, answer your phone," Sam said to Margot as another uniformed officer appeared and ushered Martin upstairs.

"Conrad?" Margot asked, breathless.

Dustin had gone limp in her grasp.

"Dead," Sam said. "Probably since we saw him this morning. Stabbed in the chest."

Margot nodded, a mix of relief and sadness coursing through her. How had everyone missed the signs that Conrad wasn't well for all those years? Dustin's words resonated in her mind, about there being certain times in a man's life that were important.

Thomas had been not quite fifteen when he died and that would mean that he would have been nearly twenty-five when Henry was taken and almost thirty when Dustin had vanished. Not the milestones she'd anticipated, but she didn't doubt they held some important significance to Conrad. It was a shame they couldn't ask him.

Sam dragged Dustin to his feet and out of Margot's embrace. "Dustin Grady, you are under arrest for the murder of Conrad Baptiste and the kidnapping and attempted murder of Martin Fairbanks. You have the right to remain silent. Anything you say can and will be used against you in a court of law. You have a right to an attorney. If you cannot afford an attorney, one will be provided for you. Do you understand these rights as I have read them to you?"

"I had to," he mumbled, as if he hadn't heard Sam's words.

Sam sighed and handcuffed him, then ushered him upstairs to a waiting patrol car. Margot followed, feeling heavy and slow. The adrenaline that had fueled her confrontation with Dustin ebbed, leaving her exhausted.

The evening air was cool on her face,

rousing her a little as red and blue lights flashed and then disappeared toward the center of town. An ambulance was parked at the bottom of the driveway, and two paramedics tended to Martin.

"Cynthia and Bernard will be relieved to know he's safe," Margot said, standing beside Sam.

"They will." Sam rounded on her. "How could you be so reckless and stupid? You could have been hurt or worse!"

"I was going to call you, but I left my phone in the car. If I'd waited, he could have hurt Martin. And I may be a minister, but I'm not helpless. Remember I got the same combat training as everyone else." Margot didn't like having to remind her cousin of her training.

"Still you aren't a soldier anymore. It's not your job to put yourself in harm's way," Sam said.

"I did what I had to. I disarmed Dustin and deescalated the situation."

"Martin got his hands on that knife. What would you have done if I hadn't shown up?"

"I would have talked him down."

Sam let out a slow exhale and pinched the bridge of her nose. "Look, I'm grateful you found them and that we got Martin back safe. It's just … stressful for me having to worry about you, too."

"I can take care of myself, Sam. I promise." She tucked her hands inside her jacket sleeves. "I'm sorry Mr. and Mrs. Grady have to learn their son is alive, only to be charged with murder."

Sam nodded.

"Did you ever follow up on Veronica?" Margot asked. She knew the reporter wasn't responsible, but she wanted to put her own suspicions to rest.

"She was friends with Conrad's ex-wife and fought to get the story of Thomas' disappearance. When the other boys went missing, she claimed them as hers too. Like it was the least she could do to honor Thomas' legacy."

"I'm glad she wasn't involved."

"I don't get why Conrad did it in the first place," Sam said, leaning against the hood of her car.

"If Dustin's to be believed, it sounds like Conrad was suffering from an undiagnosed mental illness. Dustin's story was that Conrad said God told him he had to kill his son, like the parable of Abraham and Isaac. For some reason, Conrad felt compelled to repeat the cycle with other boys that looked like Thomas. Somehow, Dustin had convinced him to let him live—only to be caught in the same cycle."

"This sort of thing shouldn't happen in Port Marie," Sam said. "We're a nice little town with no drama."

Margot smirked. "Every town has its fair

share of drama. We should have known this mystery was bound to surface again." It had taken twenty years, but her prayer had been finally answered.

"I guess I can't argue with that."

"Given that this case is wrapped up, can we have our worship space back now?" Margot asked.

Sam gave her a tired grin. "I'll make sure the crime scene gets released in the morning."

The ambulance pulled away, leaving Margot and Sam alone in front of the church. The night grew quiet and Margot studied the building, it's decades of old secrets had finally been unearthed.

"We'll get through this as a community," Margot said, realizing she'd found the topic for her next sermon.

10

By morning, Port Marie was abuzz with news of Margot's involvement in Martin's rescue. The front page of the newspaper bore a much lengthier article by Veronica Morris-Sawyer.

Port Marie Mystery Laid to Rest

By: Veronica Morris-Sawyer, Staff Writer

Twenty years have gone by since Thomas Baptiste went missing and we now have the answers Port Marie has been seeking for two decades. In total, four boys, including Thomas Baptiste, Henry Dalton, Dustin Grady, and Martin Fairbanks, were taken from their homes and around town. According to Officer Samantha Raymond, the culprit in the first three disappearances was Thomas' own father, Conrad Baptiste. Officer Raymond said, "It appears Mr. Baptiste suffered from an undiagnosed mental illness that fueled his actions. The remains of Thomas Baptiste and Henry Dalton were found in the basement of the church where Conrad had served as custodian until recently." Sources confirm that Conrad Baptiste was later found dead in his home.

In a tragic turn of events, Dustin Grady survived his abduction, only to fall victim to Conrad Baptiste's delusions. He has been arrested and awaits arraignment.

His family has a bittersweet reunion ahead of them.

Witnesses describe the rescue of Martin Fairbanks by local minister and Army veteran Margot Quade as heroic. Young Martin is quoted as saying, "She stepped in like it wasn't anything and talked him down." Martin's family couldn't be reached for comment at this time.

"You made the news," Sam said as she knocked on the door to Margot's office, much like Pedro had done only a few short days ago.

Margot set her notes aside and smiled. "I saw. I guess Veronica finally got the story she was looking for—the one that brought closure."

Sam sat down across from her. "Cynthia bawled for a good half hour when we finally let her see Martin. He couldn't stop talking about you."

"I'm glad they got a happy ending."

"I am, too."

"Did you ever figure out how Dustin managed to get Martin alone and out of the house?" Margot pressed.

"It turned out they'd been messaging online for a while. I don't think Martin realized what he was getting into. He thought he was just meeting up with a friend, someone his own age."

"I still can't believe we all missed the signs that Conrad wasn't well," Margot said, rubbing at the tight feeling in her upper chest; of regret—sadness. "He was such an integral part of this community for so long."

"Some people are really good at hiding those parts of themselves. What I don't understand is how Dustin ended up falling for his theory."

"I can't speak for him, but I got the feeling he played on Conrad's sense of remorse. After a time, Stockholm syndrome took over. In order to survive, he had to believe what Conrad believed and it became real to him."

"Tragic." Sam sighed, then asked, "Did the Daltons and Maureen Prescott decide what they wanted to do about services?"

Nodding, Margot said, "They agreed to have a small ceremony during today's worship to honor their sons' memories. Once the remains have been released, we're going to do a private graveside service for just family. I have a feeling we're going to have a packed house today. It may not have been the outcome they were hoping for, but having a resolution, closure is still a powerful thing."

"I got word that it looks like they might not charge Dustin after all," Sam said. "The prosecution is recommending he seek mental health treatment in a secure facility upstate."

"I'm thankful he'll get the help he needs after all that he's been through," Margot said.

"It's really the best outcome he could hope for."

Margot turned back to her sermon notes. "I hate to cut this short, but I need to finish getting ready for this morning's service."

"I look forward to it."

"I'll see you out there."

Sam left Margot to finish gathering her thoughts. After a few minutes, Margot donned her vestments and headed out to the pulpit. They'd set two other chairs beside the main lectern, where the local Imam and Rabbi were seated waiting for her. As she'd predicted, the pews were crammed with people. She could see that Pedro had brought out the extra folding chairs that now lined the back of the sanctuary. Even with the extra seating, some people stood, all ready to mourn the loss of two lives cut short.

"I haven't seen it this full in a long time," the Rabbi whispered as Margot took her seat and the choir began the opening anthem.

"Unfortunately, tragedy unites people," Margot murmured.

Down in front of the pulpit, two poster-sized photos of Thomas and Henry were adorned with wreaths. Two tall taper candles sat between them, their flames burning bright. Maureen Prescott sat in the front row on the right while the Daltons sat opposite her. They may have agreed to this joint memorial, but there was no denying Maureen's ex-husband was the reason why Henry Dalton was dead.

"Good morning, everyone," Margot said into the microphone when everyone had taken their seats. She faltered, searching for her next words, the sea of faces staring up at her in expectation washing over her like a wave. She cleared her throat and gripped the edges of the pulpit to steady herself.

"This morning's service is going to be a little different. As most of you know, we've had several losses to our community. We will be raising up Thomas Baptiste and Henry Dalton as we lay them to rest. We are grateful that so many of you have joined us today to remember them. The other inter-faith leaders and I will be sharing brief re-marks before we invite anyone in the congregation to share any memories they might have of Thomas and Henry."

In the middle of the crowd, Margot spotted Martin seated between his parents. His mother had a firm grasp around his shoulders, but he looked fairly well recov-ered. She was surprised he felt comfortable returning to the church so soon after his or-deal. Margot reminded herself that children were far more resilient than most adults gave them credit for.

Margot stepped back from the pulpit and allowed the Rabbi to speak his piece. It gave her time to collect her emotions. She hadn't expected to feel overwhelmed. After all, she'd presided over memorials before … but none with the weight of today's service. She let the lilt of the Rabbi's prayer lull her into a sense of calm.

The rest of the service flowed beautifully, and before long she stood at the exit of the sanctuary down to the fellowship hall, shaking hands and exchanging hugs with parishioners along with her colleagues. She spotted Maureen Prescott next in the line and Margot prepared herself.

"I'm glad you were able to join us today," she said, taking both of Maureen's hands in her own.

"You had lovely things to say about Thomas. Thank you."

"I wish I'd been able to know him better. And again, I am so very sorry for your loss."

Maureen sniffled and Margot guided her out of line to give her some privacy.

"If I'm honest," Maureen said, "I knew in my heart a long time ago that he was dead. I think some part of me even knew Conrad had done it. Back then, I thought maybe I was just being spiteful because of the divorce."

"It's not my business, but can I ask what led to your separation?"

"He became hyper-religious, going on and on, quoting the Bible."

"Any verses in particular?" Margot asked.

"I stopped paying attention after a while." Tears trickled down Maureen's cheeks. "I should have known something was wrong then."

"You did what you thought was best for your family. None of this is your fault."

"I feel horrible that so many lives were ruined because I couldn't see what was right in front of me."

Margot pulled the other woman into a tight embrace. "I know you feel guilty right now, but it will pass."

Maureen dried her eyes and made her way back into the flow of people heading down to the fellowship hall. Margot was about to rejoin her place in the receiving line when she felt a tug on her sleeve. She turned to see Martin standing in front of her.

She smiled at him. "How are you doing?"

"Better. Thank you for what you did." He innocently reached forward and wrapped his arms around her waist.

Surprised at the contact, Margot froze awkwardly, then hugged him back. "I'm glad I was in the right place at the right time."

Cynthia stepped up behind her son. "We're going to be having a talk about internet safety," she said.

Martin stepped back from Margot and hung his head in embarrassment. "I know. I can't trust people online even if they seem like friends."

Margot patted his shoulder as they, too, left the sanctuary behind. She stayed put until the last congregant had filtered out before facing the image of Christ on the cross hanging above the pulpit.

She whispered a prayer, thanking the Lord for giving her the strength to have weathered this storm. It had been an unexpected test of her faith, but she was confident she had come through stronger on the other side. Whatever came next, she knew she could face it head on.

CAST THE FIRST STONE

A REVEREND MARGOT QUADE

COZY MYSTERY NOVELLA BOOK 3

Cast the First Stone

S.E. BIGLOW

For information contact; www.sarah-biglow.com

Copyedited by: Liza Street

Proofreading and Formatting by: Under Wraps Publishing Services

Cover Design by: Deranged Doctor Design

Published by Sarah Biglow: August 2019

10 9 8 7 6 5 4 3 2 1

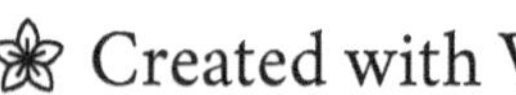 Created with Vellum

1

Summer heat rippled through the air, turning the road into a hazy wave as Margot Quade took off at a jog. The sun had barely risen above the trees, but the small town of Port Marie was under a heat advisory already. Her phone—clipped to her armband for running—showed a temperature of eighty degrees. It felt at least ten degrees hotter on the dark pavement, and it would only get worse as the day wore on. Her time in the Middle East had recalibrated what she found unbearable weather wise.

Since then she considered this temperature balmy.

She slowed to a brisk walk as she crested a hill on the outskirts of town, the forlorn outline of the Baptiste home shimmering in the distance. A 'For Sale' sign was perched high and visible at the edge of the property. She didn't blame Conrad's ex-wife for selling the place after he'd died. The town was only just getting back to normal following the revelation that Conrad had abducted and killed two boys and turned a third into his protégé.

She prided her hometown on being resilient. Her small community had endured more tragedy since her time overseas than anyone should face in a lifetime.

The chapter of the audiobook on her phone ended and she picked up the pace again, letting the downward momentum carry her toward the center of town. Just as the narrator started the next chapter, a loud noise—like a gunshot—drew Margot's attention.

She pulled the headphones from her ears and stopped, listening for a repeat. None came. She tried to gauge the direction it had come from while she stood on the road. It didn't matter, because she picked up on the sound of breaking branches in the tree line to her right. She approached the edge of the road, waiting for whoever was about to emerge.

The breaking of twigs and the crunch of underbrush grew louder, setting Margot's nerves on alert. Every muscle in her body coiled in anticipation, preparing her to jump into action. Suddenly a woman burst through the foliage, eyes glassy and bleeding profusely from her left shoulder. The wound was only a few inches from hitting her heart.

"Help me," the woman rasped before collapsing to the ground.

Margot's training kicked in and she bent

over the prone figure, scooping her into a bridal carry before taking off at a run. A memory of her time overseas threatened to overtake Margot's focus, but she pushed it down. This woman needed her here now, in the present. Margot did her best to keep pressure on the woman's wound by keeping the left side of her body pressed against her own chest. The woman's shallow breaths signaled she was clinging to life as they closed the distance to the hospital, located not far from the police and fire stations.

Given the early hour, Margot didn't encounter anyone else on the road. *This isn't the Middle East,* she reminded herself. She kept moving forward, her attention laser focused on the hospital. The woman's light frame jostled in Margot's grip. *Why is she so frail? Who would shoot her?* Margot's legs pumped a steady pace as she turned at the back of the fire station and skidded to a halt outside the hospital's emergency room entrance. She caught her breath and walked into the space.

"I need some help here," she announced loudly.

The charge nurse at the station stuck her head around the corner. The ER was quiet—not that Margot suspected it would ever be considered bustling—and this was probably the first person the nurse had seen all morning.

"What's the matter?" the nurse asked, coming into full view.

"I need a gurney. This woman's been shot," Margot said.

Her words spurred the nurse to action. She slammed her fist onto a call button on the wall before going in search of a gurney. The woman in Margot's arms moaned. Blood trickled from the corner of her mouth. Her hair was matted to her head in thick tangles and her skin was pale—too pale for this time of year.

Despite her frail appearance, she looked somehow familiar. Margot tried to place the woman's face, but came up empty.

The nurse returned with an orderly and doctor in tow, and Margot eased her charge onto the gurney. The woman refused to relinquish her grip on Margot's wrist though.

"The doctors are going to take good care of you," Margot whispered, gently prying the woman's fingers off her skin.

Margot stood immobile for a moment, watching them disappear through a door marked 'Authorized Personnel Only.' The adrenaline rush subsided and she took stock of herself. Her clothing was stained bright red with blood, as were her hands. The police needed to be notified and her current state wouldn't allow her to operate a phone. The wheels in her mind turned, still trying to place the woman in some sort of context or from a memory.

Finally, her mind filled in the gap and she

hoped it wasn't wishful thinking. *Could it really be her?* She turned to the nurse. "You need to call the police. Ask for Officer Samantha Raymond. If she's not on duty, tell them to call her anyway."

Margot claimed a spot in one of the waiting room chairs, careful not to touch anything. She knew not to contaminate anything else and preserve the evidence. The nurse returned with the offer of sweats and as the blood dried on her skin, Margot longed to clean up. She knew better. The nurse disappeared again, leaving the clothing on a chair beside Margot. Time ticked by and Margot began to doubt whether the nurse had followed through with calling the police when Sam burst into the ER, looking frazzled. She wasn't in uniform, which meant the dispatcher had called her at home. Sam spotted Margot and closed the distance between them in seconds.

"What happened? Are you okay?" Sam asked, prodding at Margot's chest and hands.

"I'm fine. It's not my blood," Margot replied, looking at the rust-colored stains drying on her skin. "I'll answer your questions, but maybe a change of clothes first?"

"Sure. I need to get a tech out here to collect your clothes." A look of relief washed over her face.

The charge nurse reappeared and approached. "The doctor is operating on her right now. He'll be out to speak with you when he's done."

"Thanks," Sam and Margot said in unison.

"Wait here just a minute," Sam said, dashing back out the way she'd come in.

Margot waited, taking in the silence

around her. After the flurry of her own entrance, the space had calmed down. The stillness was punctuated only by the periodic hiss of the air conditioning units trying to keep the place cool in the oppressive heat.

Sam soon returned, followed by a short woman with a bob carrying what Margot assumed to be an evidence collection kit.

Sam gestured for the tech to follow them into the bathroom. Margot knew the experience wasn't going to be pleasant as soon as the technician pulled out a scraping tool to collect the dried blood on her hands. Next came her shirt and pants, leaving her clad only in her underwear. It wasn't very dignified, but she dressed in the lightweight sweats quickly.

"Let's find somewhere quiet to talk," Sam said once the technician gathered her kit and left.

They settled into the hospital cafeteria after letting the nurse know where to find them. Margot downed a cup of lukewarm coffee.

"So, tell me what happened," Sam prompted.

"I was out for a run when I heard what sounded like a gunshot. I had earbuds in, still it is a pretty distinctive sound. Maybe two minutes later, a woman came stumbling out of the brush. She had what appeared to be a bullet wound in her left shoulder. She asked for help and then collapsed."

"You didn't think to call the police?"

"There wasn't time. I knew she needed medical attention. Getting her to the hospital sooner rather than later was the better move. I called once I knew she was being treated."

"Can you tell me where you found her?"

"I can do better than that. I can show you."

Sam jotted a few notes down onto her notepad. "Okay."

Margot could sense Sam's reluctance to

leave the hospital without getting to question the victim, but neither of them knew how long the doctor would be in surgery or when the woman would be allowed visitors.

"There's something else," Margot said softly.

"Yeah?"

"I didn't recognize her at first. Not until I thought about it for a while. But, Sam, I could swear she's Penelope … Penelope Van Ness."

Sam let out a snort of disbelief. "Margot, she went missing years ago."

"Believe me, I remember. She was my best friend. But I'm telling you, it's her."

"How do you know it's not Olivia? They're identical twins."

"I just know." She'd spent a lot of time with both of the Van Ness sisters growing up. She could tell them apart when most people had trouble. Both girls liked to wear their hair the same way, but Penelope's always swirled to the right while Olivia's swirled to the left. Olivia had dimples where Penelope had none. Although identical they weren't mirror twins, but a lot of their quirks seemed to be opposites.

Sam blew out a breath. "Show me where you found her. We can sort out who she is when she's awake and talking."

RETURNING to where she found the victim was faster by car. Even then, Margot was able to retrace her steps. "Stop here."

Sam pulled over to stop and they both climbed out. Margot bent over the small pool of blood that had congealed on the ground. "She definitely came from that direction. I'm not sure how far back."

"I'll get someone out to secure the scene and we'll set up a perimeter search," Sam said, just as her cell phone blared. She answered it on the second ring. "Officer Raymond."

She waited a beat, listening. Margot strained her ears, but couldn't hear the other voice.

Then Sam responded, "I'll be right there. Thank you for the call."

"News from the hospital?" Margot guessed.

"The doctor is done with surgery and wants to talk to me."

"I'll go with you."

"There won't be much for you to do. She's still out of it."

"I'll sit with her until she wakes up then. I need to know if I'm right, Sam. Please?"

"Okay." Sam radioed for backup at the scene and requested the one K-9 unit on the Port Marie police force before they headed back to the hospital.

The same nurse from before led them through the maze of first floor rooms to one at the very back of the hospital. The chart on the door read Jane Doe, but that could change soon.

The doctor waited just inside the room. Margot moved to sit by the unconscious woman's bedside and began to pray. She prayed for her to wake up and for Margot's suspicions as to her identity to be correct. Penelope and her sister Olivia's disappearance at sixteen had almost destroyed Margot's world more than Thomas Baptiste's disappearance. There'd been no trace found of either sister. From what Margot remembered, Penelope's boyfriend at the time, Rider Arthur, had been questioned about her whereabouts, but that line of inquiry had gone nowhere.

She paid just enough attention to Sam's conversation with the doctor to get the gist of the woman's condition.

"She's very lucky to be alive. A few inches to the right and she would be dead."

"She looks like she's in pretty rough shape for just a gunshot wound," Sam noted.

"She's suffering from vitamin D deficiency as well as malnutrition. Wherever she's been, it hasn't been good."

"When can I talk to her?" Sam asked.

"She's pretty heavily sedated. She'll be out for at least an hour."

"Did you recover the bullet?"

"No. It was a through and through. She got lucky with that, too." He looked over at Margot. "You were smart to get here as quick as you did."

"I had to help her. I couldn't turn down someone in need. If you don't mind, I'd like to stay with her so she's not alone when she wakes up."

"Sure. We don't know who she is though."

"I think I might have an idea," Margot said under her breath.

"We'll take her fingerprints and run them

through the missing persons database," Sam said.

"Just out of curiosity, who do you think she is?" the doctor probed. He'd clearly heard Margot's comment.

Margot shot Sam a questioning look, as if asking for permission to share her theory. Sam nodded, so Margot said, "Penelope Van Ness."

The doctor let out a whistle through his teeth. "If that's true, that would be the biggest mystery solved since the whole Conrad Baptiste thing."

He wasn't wrong. Sam pulled out her phone and approached the bed. Margot raised an eyebrow as she brought up an app on her phone and pressed the woman's fingers to the screen one at a time.

"Welcome to the twenty-first century. It's so much easier than fingerprint powder."

Margot was surprised the local police department had sprung for such high-tech gadgetry. The Chief of Police was old school from what she'd heard. Then again, crime had moved into the twenty-first century long ago. If they wanted to keep up, they needed to adapt.

"We should know soon if your hunch is right," Sam said.

The doctor cleared his throat to draw their attention. "I'll be back to check on her in a little while."

Sam leaned against the wall beside Margot's chair. "Where do you think she's been all this time?"

"I don't know." She wrapped her hands around the unconscious woman in front of her. *Where did you go, Pen? Have you been here the whole time?* "If she's alive, if it's really her, what happened to Olivia? Where is she?" Margot added.

"We weren't far from the Baptiste property, right?" Sam said, drumming her fingers against the back of her phone.

"Not far, no. But this feels different from what happened to Thomas and the other boys," Margot answered.

"Wait, I'm not saying it was him. We would have found other people in that house and I think Dustin would have mentioned a woman being kept prisoner, even in his delusional state."

Margot didn't disagree. That still didn't answer the question of where Penelope had been all this time. *Did I leave you behind?*

"But who else lives around there?" Sam muttered.

Margot ran through a mental list of the families who'd lived in the area when she was growing up. People didn't move around within Port Marie. Newer generations moved away, but their parents stayed put. She was about to answer when Sam's phone gave a prolonged beep. They both jumped at the noise and peered at the screen. The word 'Match Found' flashed in bright green text.

"Moment of truth," Sam whispered and tapped the screen.

She nearly dropped the phone. Margot was grateful she was sitting down. It was not the answer they'd been expecting. The woman lying prone before them was not Penelope Van Ness, but her sister, Olivia.

3

Margot studied the woman before them. Had time dulled her ability to tell them apart? Besides the mirrored qualities the sisters possessed, Olivia bore a scar on her right forearm from when she broke it at summer camp. She'd been so proud of her cast upon their return to school. She'd flaunted having her sister carry all of her books. Margot stood and moved to the other side of the bed, lifting the woman's arm up to the light until she found the scar in its rightful place.

"It's Olivia," Margot confirmed, pointing to the scar. "I remember when she broke her arm and got this scar. She had pins put in."

"If this is Olivia, then where is Penelope?" Sam remarked.

"If we can figure out where Olivia had ran from, maybe we'll find out."

Between them, Olivia let out a groggy moan as she began to awake. They both looked down at her and waited for her eyes to open. They were the same clear blue, if a bit dulled by the anesthesia and from time spent out of the sun. She looked first to her left, her eyes sluggish as they focused on Sam leaning against the chair. Olivia's gaze moved more quickly to the right and zeroed in on Margot's face.

"I know you," she slurred.

Hot tears pricked the back of Margot's eyes as she watched recognition dawn on her friend's face.

"Margot," she said softly.

"Olivia, this is a miracle," Margot said, grasping her friend's hand tight between her own. She looked over at Sam and gave a small nod. The doctor needed to know that Olivia was awake.

"Excuse me," Sam said and left the room.

"Was that Sam?" Olivia rasped. She winced as she tried to move in the bed.

"Yeah. We've all grown up," Margot replied. She had so many questions that needed answers, but she knew Olivia needed rest to recover from her injuries. She restrained herself from barraging her friend.

Olivia lifted her hand that was grasped in Margot's gesturing at the cross and dog tags hanging around her neck. "What's that?"

Margot brushed a finger across the cool metal. "After high school, I went into seminary. I joined the Army as a chaplain. I've been home a little while, nearly nine months now. A lot has happened."

"Tell me everything," Olivia prompted, her eyes brightening a little.

"There will be plenty of time for that," Margot replied as the door to the room swung open and Sam returned with the doctor right behind her.

At that moment, Olivia spotted the badge clipped to Sam's belt. She shrank back into the bed.

"Hey, it's okay," Margot said, feeling the woman's hand go clammy. She looked at her cousin. "I think you're making her nervous."

"I'm here to help," Sam said, holding her hands out in front of her in a placating gesture. It didn't seem to lessen Olivia's anxiety.

The doctor advanced past Sam. Olivia pressed as close to Margot as she could get without tangling herself in the monitor lines and IVs.

"Uh … doc, I think you might be the one freaking her out," Sam noted.

The doctor stopped mid-step, understanding. "Why don't I go get a nurse," he mumbled and left the room.

Olivia relaxed once he was no longer in the room. Sam pulled the chair up to the other side of the bed and sat down, pulling out her pen and notepad.

"Olivia, I'm with the police now. Margot was the one who found you. We want to help you. Do you feel up to answering some questions?"

"You didn't tell him who I was, did you?" Olivia squeaked.

Sam and Margot shared a confused look.

"He thinks you might be Penelope," Sam answered.

"You can't tell him. Please, just tell him I'm a Jane Doe."

"He knows we ran you fingerprints," Sam replied.

"Lie to him. Say they didn't match anything. Please I'm begging you."

"I'll keep it under wraps, but can you tell me why?"

Tears trickled down Olivia's cheeks. "If he knows, he'll tell other people, and then it will get around that I'm still alive."

"That's a good thing," Margot countered.

Olivia shook her head. "Please, don't tell them."

"We won't," Sam answered. After a moment, she leaned forward and asked, "Can you tell us what happened to you and Penelope?"

"I don't want to talk about it."

"Do you know who shot you?"

Olivia worried her lower lip. "I didn't see. I was running and then …"

"I think we should let her rest," Margot interrupted more forcefully than she'd intended.

"I know you've been through a lot, but if we're going to help you, we need as much as information as you can give us," Sam pressed.

Olivia shook her head. "It's all so fuzzy."

Sam sighed and stowed her notepad. Margot knew her cousin well enough to see the flicker of frustration in her gaze. She hated giving up. "I'm going to leave my card with my cell number on it. If you think of anything or want to talk, call me," Sam said. She tucked the edge of her card under the hospital phone on the bedside table.

Olivia settled back against the pillows. After a moment, she let Margot's hand go. Margot paused and pulled the chain from around her neck. She pressed it into Olivia's other hand.

"This gave me comfort when I thought there would be no light again. I hope it brings you some comfort, too."

"Thank you," Olivia whispered, tucking her arm beneath the blankets.

Margot and Sam left the hospital room.

The doctor was just returning with a nurse. He stopped them before they could get far.

"Did she give you anything useful?"

"I can't discuss what she told me. Active investigation."

He frowned. "Can you at least tell me if my patient is a Jane Doe or not?"

"Fingerprints weren't a match. She's still a Jane Doe for now. She doesn't remember her name. Might be some memory problems or maybe the anesthesia."

"Well," he said, "you might be interested to know we did a few quick x-rays to make sure that bullet wound was the only damage we were dealing with. The x-rays depict quite a few healed breaks. Some are old, possibly going back twenty years. Wherever this woman was, she was not treated well."

"Thanks for the information," Sam said, and turned to make her way to the exit.

Margot fell into step beside her. "I don't like this at all," she whispered.

"I don't either. She's been somewhere in town for twenty years. Someone knows something. She escaped but she's terrified whoever held her captive will find her and come for her."

"Can you put a uniformed officer at her door?"

"She doesn't seem to trust authority figures, or men. That said, I don't think it's a bad idea to keep her under a protective watch. I'll see if I can get a female officer to sit with her."

"What do you think happened to Penelope?" Anger and guilt constricted her chest. Anger at whoever had hurt her friends and guilt for moving on with her life when at least one sister was still within reach.

"I don't know, but I'm going to find out."

4

Margot was grateful for Sam's offer of a ride home. A shower and her own clean clothes called to her. The rest of the town was beginning to wake up, blissfully unaware that another mystery was in their midst, ready to be unraveled.

"I'm going to find out what happened to the both of them," Sam repeated as Margot climbed out of the passenger side.

"I know you will," Margot replied, already

trying to devise a way she could help without getting in Sam's way.

They parted ways and Margot dashed into the relative coolness of her apartment. The air conditioning left a little to be desired. She set the shower to be as cold as she could stand it before disrobing and climbing in.

The water washed away the physical evidence of Olivia's assault, but it flooded Margot with recollections of Olivia's and Penelope's disappearance. Penelope and Rider had been on the outs, which wasn't unusual. Of that much she was certain. Rider wasn't one to take rejection well, which was one reason Penelope had often gone back to him. He'd make some excuse for why he deserved another chance claiming he loved her or that he was sorry he'd cheated. Both Olivia and Margot had urged Penelope to sever ties with him permanently. They'd insisted that he was too controlling. But after the twins' disappearance, the police had questioned him and he'd been with friends at a party the night the sisters went missing.

At the time, Margot believed his alibi, just like everyone else had. Was that because she didn't want to believe someone her own age capable of murder? Or maybe it was because if he didn't know what happened, she wasn't alone in wondering about their fate.

Penelope and Olivia's car had been found abandoned in the woods, but there'd been no trace of them. Margot had joined the search party, combing the woods to no avail. No trace of either girl had ever been found. Or at least that's what the police had told the public and the girls' terrified parents. Still, the police didn't always share everything with the public. If there was more to unearth, Margot was going to find it.

AFTER GETTING CLEANED UP, Margot headed out into the oppressive heat again. This time, she was shielded from the heat by the cool air blasting in her car as she navigated to the spot where Olivia and her sister had last been seen two decades earlier. She parked on the shoulder of the road and stood, hands on hips at the edge of the small forest that ran along the edge of town. The first step through the underbrush sent shivers down her spine, as if she were following ghosts onward into the unknown.

In a manner of speaking, that was exactly what she was doing.

She picked her way carefully through sharp, broken branches and brambles to a small clearing near a stream that fed into a lake just a few miles away. It was secluded, but it was where the search party for the Van Ness girls had ended up. She thought she remembered that the K-9 unit had tracked their scent here, but had then lost it.

"Where did you go?" she murmured to the emptiness around her.

No answer just silence, not that she expected a response. But she did catch a glimpse of a structure through the foliage across the stream. Her mind urged her to recall why it felt so familiar. Much like that morning when it took her longer than she wanted to remember Olivia and Penelope, it was too slow coming to her. She retrieved her phone from her pocket and turned on the map function. The tiny blinking dot appeared in the middle of the wooded area, orienting her.

"Maybe," she mumbled to herself, letting her mind wander—Rider and his family lived not far from here.

She didn't need to look up the address. The house number and street name had been cemented in her memory by the frequency she or Olivia had to go drag Penelope away for dinner or to pick her up after one of her and Rider's fights. She plugged the address into the map function and plotted a walking course from her current location to their house.

As she'd suspected, it was a pretty straight shot from where she stood to the structure in the distance. If she'd managed to figure that out now, surely the police had seen the connection back then. The word around town had been that Rider had been at a party all night with his brother. But memories were faulty, especially when drinking was involved. And whether their parents knew it or not, both Rider and his brother, Trent, had been heavy drinkers in high school. It was one of the many reasons Rider and Penelope had fought. He was not a nice person under the influence—a mean drunk.

She could hear Sam's voice in the back of her mind urging her to go to the police with what she now suspected. She needed something more concrete than a hunch though, so Margot found the shallow part of the stream and waded across. As she broke through the woods on the other side of the water, she wondered if the water had disturbed the scent trail for the dogs all those years ago.

Two trucks sat in the driveway to the Arthur home. Neither looked like they were new and had likely not seen repair in years. In fact, she hadn't heard anyone mention seeing either Mr. or Mrs. Arthur in some time, let alone their sons. The house was a two-story much like many of the homes in Port Marie. Dark brown siding made it blend into the surroundings like camouflage. It hadn't changed since she'd been there last. Margot crossed to the weed-covered front walk and the tiny hairs on the nape of her neck stood on end. She did not have good memories of being at this house. She was halfway up the walk when the front door opened and a scruffy, unshaven man with a receding hairline appeared.

"This is private property," he barked.

Margot stopped.

"I'm sorry. I got a little turned around," Margot said. She still wasn't wholly comfortable with lying, but she couldn't gauge how the man before her would react to seeing her again. She hadn't seen him in nearly two decades, but she recognized Rider. His blue-gray eyes still carried a hint of distrust.

"Road's that way. Get gone before I call the police."

"You probably don't remember me. Margot Quade. We went to school together. I was friends with Penelope and Olivia Van Ness," Margot said, gambling on whether he'd continue talking to her.

He squinted at her and then gave her a sneer. "Oh, I remember you all right. Heard you took off as soon as graduation was over."

"I joined the Army," she said. He didn't

need to know she was a chaplain. With a man like him, displaying as much as power as possible was better. It told him that she could take care of herself.

"Right. Well, this is still private property. If you don't want me to call the cops, you'll turn around and leave."

Margot held up her hands. "No need to do that."

She started to back up when she caught sight of someone peering out the picture window in the living room. She could swear it was a little girl.

Had Rider married and had a child? Or perhaps his brother still lived there and the girl was his daughter? She mulled over the child's identity as she retraced her steps back to her car.

She settled behind the wheel and cranked the air, letting it clear her head. She hit speed dial three on her phone, waiting for Sam to answer.

"You've reached Sam Raymond, leave a message." Margot hung up without leaving a message. She had another avenue she could follow to at least identify the child before reaching out to her cousin again. She just hoped it would work.

5

She headed straight to the Port Marie Public Library. She could get what she needed on her own computer, but it felt somehow safer and more anonymous to do it on the library computer. That way, if someone noticed she was snooping, they couldn't tie it back to her.

The library was empty except for a sleepy librarian sitting at the reference desk, languidly flipping through a magazine. He didn't even look up as Margot walked in and made a beeline for the computer terminals.

She pulled up the town's vital records from the town hall website and searched *Rider Arthur* for marriage records. None came up. She went back to the main search page and tried *Trent Arthur*. One match appeared.

Eight years ago, Trent Arthur married one Darlene Cavanagh. The record indicated that Darlene had been 26 at the time of her marriage—young enough that Margot wouldn't have recognized her from school.

She'd barely caught a glimpse of the girl in the window, but Margot thought the dates lined up about right. Town birth records were harder to access than marriage licenses, because they weren't kept the same way. There was one person she might be able to ask to get an idea.

First, though, she needed to let Sam know what she'd discovered. The line rang five times and Margot held her breath, waiting for the message to click over again and send her to voicemail.

"Hello?" Sam said.

"Sam, hi. I tried to call before but it went to voicemail. Is this a bad time?"

"No. The techs just came in from the field. They were able to track the trail to the middle of the woods, but then they lost it."

"I may have someone you should talk to."

"Really? I thought I told you I was handling this," Sam said with only a hint of annoyance.

From her tone, Margot guessed Sam wasn't going to refuse help on this one. They'd both been invested in the Van Ness sisters' disappearance. "I just tried to retrace their steps from twenty years ago."

"You know the police combed that area back when they first disappeared, right? They didn't find anything then, either."

"There was a stream running near the spot where the dogs lost the scent. What if the water threw them off?"

"Why do I get the feeling you crossed the stream?"

"The spot abutted a piece of property. You want to guess who it belonged to?"

"Please don't say the Arthurs," Sam said with an exasperated groan.

"Right in one," Margot said in a hushed tone, even though the librarian wasn't paying attention.

Sam sighed. "We've been over this. They weren't involved."

"Because friends of theirs said they were at a party? Despite wanting to believe the best in people," Margot said, "I know that people are flawed. They lie. You and I both know that Rider and Trent were anything but model citizens back then."

"Spare me the sermon, okay? Just tell me you didn't go to the house."

When Margot didn't answer right away, Sam let out another groan. "Margot, seriously. What were you thinking?"

"I just walked by. I saw Rider. He wasn't happy to have anyone—especially an old friend of his ex-girlfriend—on his property. And I saw a little girl there, too. Do you know if Trent still lives on the property?"

"Look, I don't like Rider or his brother, either. They were total jerks in high school and he wasn't good for Penelope. But you need to stay away from them. Promise me."

"Okay. I won't go near them, promise."

"Good. I've got to go," Sam muttered, ending the call.

Margot looked at her phone. She would stay away from Rider and Trent, but she had no intention of dropping her search for that little girl's identity. She couldn't shake the feeling that whoever the girl was, she wasn't safe.

She could ask Olivia, but given her friend's reluctance to share any details about her captivity, Margot suspected Olivia would be just as tight-lipped about the child if she knew anything at all.

Margot left the comfort and solitude of the library. She drove the block and a half to the elementary school. She had an old friend who might be able to shed some light on this mystery.

The school year was still in session, which meant teachers—including her old friend, Wanda Lawrence—stayed late at the end of the day. Margot had known Wanda since kindergarten. She hadn't been surprised to learn that Wanda had become a teacher and stayed close to home.

Margot checked in at the front desk—the receptionist was one of her congregants who was there every Sunday like clockwork—and got directions to Wanda's classroom. She wove around students eager to be free for the summer as they darted out of classrooms down the hall to the front of the school. She found Wanda saying goodbye to some of her fourth-grade students. Given that Margot had seen the child only a few short hours ago, she didn't expect to find her here.

"Margot!" Wanda exclaimed, pulling her into a tight hug. "This is a surprise."

"I felt bad about not getting to see you sooner," Margot said. Yes, she had ulterior motives for seeing her old friend, but she did feel guilty for not having made an effort to track her down before now.

"Let me just get these guys on the bus, and then we can chat."

"Of course."

Margot stepped into the classroom and waited while Wanda ushered the kids out to their bus to take them home. She admired the hand-drawn pictures and poems pinned on the wall.

"They're a good group," Wanda said, appearing in the doorway.

"You must be so proud of them." Margot gestured at the walls.

"I am. But, it's even better when they can take pride in their own work." Wanda came the rest of the way into the classroom and started straightening her desk. "So, how've you been?"

"It's been an adjustment. I've been back almost nine months now and some days I think I'm all settled into the flow of civilian life. Other days, I'll hear a sound or see something out of the corner of my eye that reminds me of my time overseas."

"You were just a chaplain," Wanda noted in a dismissive tone.

"That doesn't mean I didn't witness my fair share of horrible things." It took time to adjust, too. She thought of Derek Nesbit. He'd finally settled into his new life with his wife, Catalina. They would be welcoming a baby boy in a mere few months. Margot had found her new calling at the church, but sometimes she wasn't sure she'd really settled into life back home.

"Of course. I'm sorry, I didn't mean to trivialize what you went through."

"It's okay. I have someone to talk to," Margot assured her. Reverend Hawley had become something of a therapist to her since her return and she was grateful for his counsel.

"I keep meaning to go to church, but I just can't seem to get myself moving Sunday mornings," Wanda said, averting her gaze.

"Finding time for faith can be hard. But also, it could be you don't need to be in a spiritual space to feel close to God," Margot said.

"Maybe," Wanda said. "So, have you been up to anything else recently?"

Wanda had to know how involved Margot had been in the saving of Martin Fairbanks and solving that mystery. "Nothing really. I was looking through some old school things, reminiscing about when we were in high school. It got me thinking about Penelope and Olivia Van Ness."

Wanda's face fell. "That was such a horrible time. I still can't believe they never found out what happened to them."

"I know," Margot said, biting her tongue. She'd promised to protect Olivia's secret. "It also got me thinking about Rider Arthur. I guess with being gone, I missed his brother getting married?"

"Oh, yeah. She was a bit younger than him at the time."

"They must have started a family by now," Margot suggested.

Wanda's brow furrowed. "I don't think so. At least not that I've heard of."

"What about Rider? I know he was broken up about their disappearance. Did he ever move on?"

"You know, this is going to sound horrible and like I'm such a gossip, but their parents passed away before Trent got married.

Word is they inherited the house and they both still live there. Rider sort of withdrew from town life after graduation."

He'd been aware enough to have known that Margot had left town. "That's too bad."

"The town is better off, if you ask me." Wanda leaned in closer. "I know both of them said they were at a party the night the girls vanished. But I was actually at the party they claimed to be attending. I was there all night … they weren't there."

"I'm sure there was drinking going on," Margot countered.

"Oh yeah. A lot. But I was the designated driver."

"Did you tell the police that?" Margot probed.

"Of course, I did but I guess they didn't believe me."

"Do you think someone lied to the police for them?"

Wanda arched a brow. "Teddy Nord was

best friends with Rider. I know this sounds awful, but I heard a rumor that Rider paid him off to tell the police he was there."

Margot had long suspected the Arthur brothers weren't present at the party that fateful night, but she didn't think they would resort to paying someone off—or worse, engaging in blackmail—to secure an alibi.

She needed to see Olivia again. Maybe now she would be more willing to talk, without the hovering medical staff and the police seeking answers.

6

The hospital was busier now that the afternoon shift was in full swing. Margot armed with a bouquet of flowers made her way back to the room where they'd put Olivia after her surgery. A nurse spotted Margot and moved to intercept her.

"Visiting hours are almost over."

"That's okay. I just came to drop these off for a patient," Margot replied and inclined the vase toward the door to Olivia's room.

"The Jane Doe?"

"I brought her in this morning. I thought the flowers might brighten things up and help her feel better."

"Just be quick."

"In and out," Margot replied, and backed into the room.

Afternoon sunlight filtered through the gauzy curtains, casting the room with bands of light. Olivia was propped up against a pillow. A tray of soup and Jell-O rested on a rolling table across the bed in front of her.

"I thought you might like some company," Margot said, setting the flowers on the bedside table.

"I forgot how much I don't like hospitals," Olivia said, failing to suppress a shudder.

Margot gave her a sympathetic look and sat down beside the bed. "I'm guessing you haven't gotten much rest."

"They keep asking me if I remember who I am. I don't know how much longer I can keep lying to them," Olivia answered in a whisper.

"I know you're scared, and I can't imagine what you've been through. I want to help you. Please, let me help."

"I don't know what you want me to say," Olivia said, looking away.

"Tell me what happened that night."

"I can't."

"Because you don't want to, or because you can't remember?" Margot pressed.

"It hurts too much."

"But if you keep it to yourself then Penelope will never get the justice she deserves."

Olivia let out a bitter laugh. "Justice? You think she deserves justice?"

"I do."

"So, I guess you don't consider suicide a mortal sin?"

"What does that have to do with anything?" Margot asked. The realization hit her too late. She sank back in the chair. "You're saying she killed herself?"

"That night, she and Rider had a huge fight. Like, their biggest ever. She said she was going to leave him for good this time. He knocked her around. She came home crying, but she wouldn't tell me what was wrong. She snuck out before I realized she was gone." Olivia took a deep, shuddering sigh. "That's when I found the note. It wasn't to our parents or anything. Just to me. I can still remember it word for word."

"I had no idea. Why didn't she talk to someone?"

"Because she was done talking," Olivia said bitterly.

"What did it say? The note?"

"She was sorry she'd caused me so much pain but that it would be over soon because she was going to get him back for everything that he'd done to her." Tears welled up in her eyes, but she fought to keep them from falling. "I knew they used to go to this place near his house when they wanted to be alone. I took a guess and I found her there. But so did he."

"Rider was there."

"Oh yeah. He got there just in time to see her shoot herself in the head. He grabbed the gun—God, I don't even know where she got it—and said he'd shoot me if I didn't help him cover it up."

Margot wanted so badly to pull her friend into a hug, but she needed to keep Olivia talking. She'd spent so long not knowing what had happened to her best friends. "So, you moved her and then what? Why wouldn't you just go home or to the police?"

"I wanted to go to the police, but by that point, Trent was in the picture. He had some twisted thought that I could replace Penelope. He got it in his brother's head that it would be easier to make people believe we both just ran away. Everyone knew we were inseparable."

"You need to tell all of this to Sam," Margot said, getting to her feet.

"Why, so she can arrest me, too?"

"Don't be ridiculous. You were under duress and then they abducted you. You're the victim here. She'll see that."

"Margot, please, no police. I told you what happened. I've been carrying that weight around for a really long time. Please just keep it between us."

"I can't do that."

"Isn't there some sort of privilege between a priest and a parishioner?"

"I think we both know that little girl is still in danger," Margot said, ignoring her question.

Olivia's tears fell now, turning her cheeks glossy and red. Her lower lip trembled. She didn't deny the girl's existence. "You don't understand what they'll do," she whimpered.

"Then tell me. I swear I want to help you, Liv. I couldn't save you both back then, but I can protect you now," Margot begged, her voice strangled by years of pent-up frustration and sorrow.

"I can't," Olivia said again.

Margot took several deep breaths to calm herself. It wouldn't do anyone any good if she let her anger overtake her. Instead, she reached over and took Olivia's free hand. "I am going to do everything I can to help you."

Olivia's whimpering turned silent as she lay back against the pillows. Margot knew their conversation was over. She also wasn't sure how much longer she could get away with being in her room before the nurse shooed her away.

Sam needed to know the whole story, no matter Olivia's apprehension. When she stepped into the hallway, she found it devoid of people.

She took quick steps to reach the parking

lot. Once there, the tiny hairs on her arms and the nape of her neck stood on end. She looked around trying to find the source of her unease, but nothing jumped out at her. That should have been her first clue things were about to take a turn for the worse.

7

As soon as she was out of the hospital, Margot pulled out her cell phone and dialed Sam. She waited while Sam's cell rang, drumming the fingers of her free hand on the steering wheel.

"Please tell me you didn't do anything else stupid," Sam said in an exasperated tone.

"I haven't gone near the Arthurs, if that's what you mean," Margot replied.

"Why do I get the feeling you aren't just calling to say hi, though?"

"I paid Olivia a visit," Margot said. "I figured she could use the company. I need to tell you what she told me. I'll meet you at the diner off Main Street."

"I'll see if I can get away," Sam said.

Margot pulled out of the parking lot and onto the street. She put the phone on speaker and set it in the cupholder beside her seat. "You need to find a way to meet me, Sam. She told me about what happened all those years ago."

"Okay, I'll be there."

Margot came to a stop at a crosswalk. The tiny hand blinked the end of a walk cycle, like the hand of a child waving. The image of the little girl in the window flashed before her eyes. "Have you been able to find anything else about who attacked her?"

The line was quiet. Then, "We don't really have much evidence to go on. No bullet means we can't even match it to a type of gun. And with Olivia refusing to talk, we're at a dead end."

Margot pressed on the gas, continuing on her trek to the diner. She was about to express her understanding for her cousin's frustration when she noticed a pair of headlights in her rearview mirror. It was still light enough that headlights weren't needed. They flashed, temporarily blinding her.

She tried to blink the black spots out of her eyes. Her car swerved into the oncoming lane of traffic and she yanked hard on the steering wheel to right herself. A car sped past her in the opposite lane, horn blaring angrily. Margot's heart beat faster in her chest as her vision resolved. Blowing out a breath, she settled back against her seat in time to feel the front bumper of the vehicle behind her slam into her back bumper, sending a resounding "crunch" through the rest of her car.

"What was that?" Sam asked, still on the line.

"Someone just hit me from behind,"

Margot replied. She pressed down on the gas and her car shot forward. The vehicle behind her kept up though, inching closer and closer.

"Sam, I think they're trying to hit me on purpose," Margot said before the car hit her again, sending her spinning out of control.

Her head smacked into the window and everything went dark.

A PROLONGED BLARE roused Margot from her stupor. She blinked. Her vision was tinged with red. Her ears rang with the distant rat-tat-tat of gunfire. Through the haze she reached out, searching for her fellow soldiers. Derek Nesbit had been sitting beside her moments earlier, but her fingers grasped only empty air. Private Peter Abrams had been at the helm but he, too, had vanished.

Margot blinked again, the present came flooding back to her.

She was no longer trapped in the ambush that had cost a young man his life. She was in her car in Port Marie, trapped between her seat and the airbag that had deployed on impact. Her chest ached and her head throbbed. She tried to clear her head. The memory of being hit from behind came back to her. She wiped at her eyes, and her fingers came away red and sticky with blood. Groping for her phone, she could just make out that Sam was still on the line.

"Sam," Margot rasped.

"I'm coming to you. Stay put," Sam's voice crackled over the line.

"Not a problem," Margot mumbled as the world started to fade at the edges.

Stay awake. Must stay awake.

She came to again as her body ached at being moved. She winced as a paramedic slid a collar around her neck and eased her onto a stretcher.

Sam hovered over her, color drained from her face in fear.

"I'm here," she said and grabbed Margot's hand.

"Headlights," Margot mumbled.

"Just rest," Sam said and kept a grip on her hand the whole way to the ambulance and during the drive to the hospital.

As her wits came back to her in the ambulance, the aches in her body began to make sense. She realized the whiplash in her neck was from being rear-ended. The throb in her chest and ribs was probably from the impact of the airbag. At least it didn't seem like anything was broken.

"Do you know what day it is?" the paramedic asked her as he took her blood pressure.

"Monday," Margot replied.

"Can you tell me your name?"

"Margot Quade."

"Good."

They pulled up to the emergency entrance to the hospital, much like Margot had done earlier. She was patient as they rolled her out of the ambulance. Sam remained at her side the entire way, glaring at anyone who got in their way. The nurse Margot had seen earlier tentatively approached and gave Margot a raised eyebrow.

"Do we have a problem?" Sam snapped, flashing her badge.

"No, Officer. I just thought I saw her earlier."

"Maybe you did. Right now, she needs medical treatment."

The doctor treating Olivia ushered them into an empty bay in the ER.

"I'm okay," Margot said, but she winced as they pressed on her side and chest.

"You might have some fractures from the airbag," the doctor said. "We're going to get you an x-ray and we'd like to keep you overnight to make sure there aren't any signs of a concussion."

"Whatever you think is best," Margot replied, her body was too sore to disagree.

Once a nurse had bandaged the cut over Margot's eye, the medical staff left her alone. Sam remained and sat down beside the bed.

"You scared me." Color had finally started to come back to her face.

"I'm sorry. I didn't mean to," Margot said with a laugh that turned into a wince. *Fractured ribs*, she reminded herself.

"What were you thinking?"

"That I was going to meet my cousin for dinner," she replied.

"Did you get a look at the driver or the car?"

Margot closed her eyes and tried to recall any details about the vehicle. The only thing she recalled clearly was the headlights flashing at her. "Just that they had their headlights on. They flashed them at me and they must have been high beams because they blinded me."

"Were they mounted on top of the car? Like a truck?"

'They could have been. Honestly, I didn't get a good look."

"I'm sure the techs can get something from your car."

Margot let out a groan. "How bad is the damage?"

"You definitely have some dents that will need to be worked out, but I think they can probably fix it."

"Thank God."

"Do you have any idea who might have done this?"

Margot had a very good idea, but Sam wasn't going to like it. "It probably has something to do with our friend we brought in this morning." She couldn't be sure who was listening. The curtains around her bed in the ER only afforded so much privacy.

Sam let out a long breath between her teeth. "I warned you."

"I know you did. And I swear to you, I didn't go back there."

"But you did some digging."

"I saw a little girl while I was on their property. I checked marriage records and Trent got married about eight years ago. I couldn't find anything about them having a child, so I asked a friend of mine if they knew anything."

"Which friend?"

"Wanda Lawrence. She's a fourth-grade teacher at the elementary school. She doesn't think she's ever seen a child with the last name Arthur come through the school."

"So, that made you suspicious," Sam concluded.

"I knew that Olivia had to know who the little girl was."

"Did she tell you?"

"No. But, she did tell me what happened the night they disappeared. That's what I was coming to tell you."

Sam leaned forward, propping her elbows on her thighs. "I'm not going to like this, am I?"

"No. But, you need to know anyway."

"Okay. Let me hear it."

Margot shifted in the hospital bed, trying to find a comfortable position for her bruised body. "Penelope and Rider had gotten into a huge fight. She was leaving him for good, but she wasn't happy. According to Olivia, Penelope slipped out of the house and left her sister a suicide note. Olivia understandably panicked and managed to track Penelope down to where the police lost the trail all those years ago. Rider found them, too. Right when Penelope took her own life."

"I'm so sorry," Sam said and squeezed Margot's hand.

"She said that Trent showed up and threatened to kill Olivia if she didn't help them hide Penelope's body. Olivia didn't go into detail after that, but I got the feeling they kept her hostage all this time to keep her quiet."

"You were right, then. They were involved."

"I don't know if they pulled the trigger, but they definitely buried Penelope's body and lied to the police. Wanda thinks Teddy Nord took a bribe to lie to the police and give the brothers an alibi for that night. She also said she didn't see them at the party and told the police but they didn't take her seriously."

"Would you be willing to swear on an affidavit to give us probable cause to search their property?"

"Of course. But I still think Olivia is hiding something. Something to do with that little girl."

"If there's a child in danger there, we'll get her out safe. I just wish Olivia had given you more information so we knew what we were walking into," Sam said, just as an orderly appeared to take Margot for x-rays.

"Please try to leave her out of it," Margot urged, careful not to say Olivia's name.

Sam knew who she was talking about. "I'll do what I can, but at some point, she won't be able to hide anymore."

8

By the next morning, Margot was in less pain thanks to the medication. She hadn't broken any bones by some miracle, but she would be bruised for a while. She could handle that. She would, however, need some help getting home now that she'd been discharged. She walked out of the hospital entrance and found not Sam, but Wanda waiting for her.

"I heard you might need a ride," Wanda said.

Margot's brow furrowed, pulling on the stitches above her eye. "You talked to Sam?"

"She mentioned you'd had an accident," Wanda answered.

"Is that all she mentioned?" Margot sensed Wanda wanted to say more. Also she wasn't sure what would have prompted Sam to tell Wanda about her car accident. Yes, she and Margot had been friends as children, but aside from the day before, they hadn't spoken in years. *You're overthinking things.*

"Is there something else she should have told me?" Wanda tucked a few strands of dark hair behind her ear.

"No. But you know family. Sometimes they say things they shouldn't."

"Come on. Let's get you settled at home."

Margot kept an eye on the side mirror for the entire trip to her apartment. She wasn't prone to a lot of paranoia—she'd made great strides in leaving the hypervigilance of war behind her—but she couldn't shake the idea that someone was watching her. Wanda got out of the car and walked with Margot, who hurried into the building and locked her apartment door as soon as they were both inside.

"Excuse the mess," Margot said realizing she'd left some dirty dishes in the sink.

"Your definition of mess and mine are quite different," Wanda said with a laugh.

"You don't have to stay. I can get settled on my own," Margot said.

"I'm under strict orders from Sam to keep you company until she can get over here."

"She has to work. And I'm sure you have a lot of end-of-the-year things to take care of. Report cards and such," Margot said, trying to usher the other woman out of her space.

"Nope. Come on, let's get you settled on the couch. Do you have any extra pillows?"

"In the bathroom closet," Margot answered, resigned to let her old friend take care of her.

She was used to taking care of herself. Yes, she was almost certain she'd been run off the road by one of the Arthur brothers. They had wanted to keep her quiet, but they hadn't succeeded. Still would they try again?

"Here you go," Wanda said and slid the extra pillow around Margot until she was propped up by softness.

"Thanks."

"If you don't mind me asking, what happened?" Wanda probed.

"I was hit from behind."

"Oh, really. Is the other driver okay?"

"I don't know." She studied Wanda's expression, clearly conveying worry. "I didn't know that you and Sam still kept in touch."

"Um, I guess she heard that you had stopped by to see me, and she figured you could use a friendly face."

"Okay."

Something still felt off about Wanda's presence. Wanda hovered in the space between the living room and the kitchen, watching Margot like a hawk. It seemed like she was afraid Margot would make a move and she'd miss it. No matter how much progress she'd made in tamping down on seeing danger around every corner, those instincts screamed at her. She couldn't just ignore them even if she tried.

"You know, I think I need to go to the bathroom," Margot announced. She managed to get herself out of the nest of pillows before Wanda could cross the room.

"Need any help?"

"No, I'm okay. Thanks though."

Margot took the long way to the bathroom, stopping in the kitchen to pick up her phone. She darted into the bathroom as fast as her injuries would allow her. She would have locked the door behind her, but the lock was broken. She called Sam and waited.

As the line rang, she made a show of letting the faucet drip, then she flushed the toilet. Her heart beat an uneven rhythm as she feared her cousin wouldn't answer.

Sam picked up immediately. "Hey, I just heard they discharged you. Need a ride home?"

"I need to know one thing," Margot whispered.

"Are you okay? Why are you whispering?"

Margot ignored Sam's questions. "Did you call Wanda to pick me up? Yes or no."

"No. Why would I do that? Besides, I literally just asked if you needed a ride."

Cold sweat began to drip down the back of Margot's neck. She'd been right to be suspicious of Wanda's presence.

"Hey, are you still there?" Sam's voice came over the line.

"Get to my place now. I think I'm in trouble." She ended the call, tucked the phone in her pocket, and turned the water on higher.

She ran her hands under the faucet just as the door to the bathroom opened and Wanda filled the space.

"Who were you talking to?" Wanda's lips were pursed into a tight line.

"Sorry?" Margot played dumb.

"You were talking to someone just now."

Margot shook her head. "I was talking to myself. Well, praying, really. My injuries could have been so much worse."

"But I heard another voice."

"It was just me. You know, do you think you could put some water on to make us some tea?"

Margot shuffled back toward the living room, leaving Wanda to stare after her.

"Of course," Wanda finally said, recovering from whatever suspicions she'd had.

Margot propped herself up on the pillows and said a real prayer that Sam would make it before Wanda did something that Margot couldn't come back from.

"Do you want anything in it?" Wanda called from the kitchen.

"Just plain," Margot answered. That way, she might have a chance of detecting anything that shouldn't be in her tea.

Silence encompassed the small apartment and Margot waited. Tension started to tighten her neck muscles, which only made the rest of her body hurt more. She wanted more of the pain medication the doctor had given her, but she knew the pills would cloud her thoughts. She needed to remain sharp. She could hear Wanda puttering around in the other room. There was something she should remember about Wanda and her connection to the Van Ness sisters. What was it though?

A loud knock on the door interrupted Margot's train of thought. She started to get up, but heard Wanda's footsteps move that way. She hoped it was Sam coming to her rescue.

"Oh, what are you doing here?" Wanda asked the unknown visitor.

"Well, Margot's my family," Sam's voice answered.

Margot let out a breath and forced herself to get to her feet.

Sam continued, "Anyway, I'm here to check up on her. Make sure she's following the doctor's orders."

"Oh, she's asleep," Wanda lied.

Margot rounded the short distance into the kitchen. "Thanks for coming, Sam."

As Wanda stood between them—it hit Margot—Wanda had been Trent's on-again, off-again girlfriend during high school. Margot was beginning to suspect that Wanda's story about Teddy wasn't true. Maybe Wanda had been the one accepting a bribe.

"You really don't need to check up on her. It's fine," Wanda said, her voice squeaky with anxiety.

"Actually, I do," Sam said in a hard voice.

"See, someone tried to hurt her yesterday. Someone who thinks she knows something about a woman who's supposed to be missing, maybe even presumed dead."

"What are you talking about?"

Margot spoke up. "I know you and Trent Arthur were in a relationship back in high school. Sam didn't call you to pick me up. So how did you know I was at the hospital? Did Trent call you? Was he the one who ran me off the road?"

The questions just fell over themselves trying to get out of Margot's mouth. Anger and fear were making her talk faster than usual.

Wanda glanced between them, looking very much like a trapped animal. Finally, resigned to the situation her shoulders slumped. The tea kettle whistled and Margot pulled it off the burner before it could distract them.

"He was a friend," Wanda said. "He just

wanted to know if you were okay."

"No, he didn't," Sam snapped.

"Okay, he didn't. He just called me because he knew I used to be friends with you," she said. "He thought you'd trust me."

"What was he hoping you'd achieve?" Margot pressed.

"I was just supposed to keep an eye on you so you wouldn't bother him anymore."

"Bother him? He held a woman captive for two decades," Margot said, her fear and irritation growing.

"He never said anything about kidnapping anyone. I swear. He just didn't want you on his property."

Margot looked to Sam. "Did you get that warrant yet?"

Sam looked at her phone. "It just came through."

"I'm coming with you. I'm not going to let them think I'm afraid of them," Margot said.

"You can't be involved. Besides, you're in no shape to be knocking down doors," Sam argued.

"That child is going to need someone to look after her."

"What are you talking about?" Wanda wailed.

Margot and Sam exchanged surprised looks. "You can't tell me you don't know about her," Margot said.

"I swear I don't know anything about a child." Wanda's eyes widened and she looked to Margot. "Wait, that's why you asked me if Trent and his wife ever had a child."

Margot could only nod.

Sam blew out a breath and pulled a pair of handcuffs from her belt. "Wanda, I'm placing you under arrest for obstruction of justice." Wanda didn't resist as Sam tightened the cuffs around her wrists. To Margot, she said, "You can come along, but you're staying in the car until we know what's going on."

9

Riding in the passenger seat of the squad car, Margot put on a brave face as the pain in her body intensified. Wanda sat handcuffed in the backseat. Margot still couldn't shake the worry that Olivia wasn't safe in the hospital. Next to her, Sam balanced her phone on one leg as she sped through the intersection by the hospital, heading toward the Arthur property.

"This is Officer Raymond, I have reason to believe a child's life is in imminent danger.

Send back-up to the Arthur property now, and I want uniforms sitting on the Jane Doe in the hospital."

"Shouldn't you drop her off at the precinct?" Margot commented, gesturing toward Wanda in the backseat.

"No time," Sam answered, pulling the car into a sharp turn at the bottom of the Arthur's driveway.

One of the trucks was missing—which lent credence to Margot's theory that one of the brothers had run her off the road. Clearly, they knew something was going on.

Before Sam could even open the driver side door, a gunshot rang out.

"Get down," Sam ordered.

Margot's reflexes kicked in and she let instinct and training take over. She had to hold herself back, reminding herself that Sam was the one with the badge and authority, not her.

"Port Marie Police. Hold your fire!" Sam

called through the rolled down window of the squad car.

Silence answered her order. Just as Sam eased her door open, another shot from the front of the house rang out, kicking up bits of dirt and gravel right in front of the car.

"I can't see who's shooting," Sam said with a huff.

Margot craned her neck—regretting the movement immediately—and peeked out of her window. She could see a first-floor window open and the muzzle of a shotgun sticking out, but the shooter's face wasn't visible.

"It's coming from that window, two o'clock," Margot said, and gestured toward the right side of the house.

Sam trained her weapon on the window just as a siren wailed and a car screeched to a halt behind them. She scooped up her radio and said, "We're taking fire from the right side of the house."

"Copy," a voice said through the radio.

Margot watched as two officers eased the doors to their vehicle open, training their weapons on the window. Another shot rang out, kicking up dirt between the two police cars. Sam ducked below the window of the driver-side door and crept around the back of car.

"Why are they shooting?" Wanda whined from the backseat.

"Obviously they don't want us here," Margot replied. She caught sight of Sam inching around the second car from the side mirror.

"I swear, I didn't know anything about a child," Wanda said feeling guilty.

"Did you know they'd locked up a woman against her will for two decades?" Margot's tone was sharp, but she couldn't stop the anger from bubbling over.

She and Wanda had been friends. She'd known Penelope and Olivia. Their family had suffered so much loss and there was still so much more the Van Nesses didn't know about their daughters' fate. It made Margot question her faith just a little. Maybe now was the right time for righteous anger.

"What woman?" Wanda asked. "What are you talking about?"

Margot suspected this entire situation would be resolved soon and Olivia could be reunited with her family. At least they could get one daughter back. It wouldn't hurt to share what Margot knew. "Trent and Rider held Olivia Van Ness captive for two decades."

"No, they didn't. She and Penelope disappeared. They ran away.'

"Is that what Trent told you when he asked you to convince Teddy to lie to the police about where they were that night?"

Wanda's mouth opened and closed several times. "He was really drunk that night. He didn't remember much of anything so it was easy to get him to tell the police he saw them at the party."

"Have you been paying him off all this time?"

"No. Trent made the payments. But … I accepted them, too."

"If you believed they ran away, why cover for Trent and Rider? If you didn't think they did anything wrong, why would you lie?" The betrayal burned in Margot's throat like acid.

"You don't understand. I loved Trent. I had wanted him to notice me. And for a while, he did. And he's not been able to forget about me all this time. Even after he married that … that child," Wanda answered, the last word coming out like poison.

Margot did her best to turn around and face Wanda so she didn't strain her bruised ribs or her neck. "You had to know Trent wasn't a nice guy."

"We can't help who we fall for. I swear, I

had no idea they'd taken Olivia. I mean, that doesn't even make sense. Rider was in love with Penelope."

"Penelope's dead." Margot tried to scan the property for any sign of a burial spot. She couldn't see anything in the front yard. She did see Sam making a mad dash around the side of the house.

The shooting ceased and Margot held her breath. Just because the shooter had retreated didn't mean they weren't still armed and hiding inside the house. And Sam had gone in without any protective gear.

Suddenly, more shots rang out, short and controlled. If Margot was right, they did not come from the shotgun. Anxiety and her training were itching to take over and go to her cousin's rescue. But she knew that Sam would be furious if Margot broke police protocol. She was here as a courtesy and because they were family. She only hoped the shots came from Sam and not from whoever had been shooting at the police.

"Requesting additional back-up at the Arthur property," a voice called over the radio sitting in the center console.

That couldn't be a good sign. At least it wasn't a call for an 'Officer Down.' Margot caught signs of movement on the first floor of the house and started to heave a sigh of relief when a truck—one she hadn't seen on her last visit to the property—sped past the two squad cars from the back of the property and zoomed off down the road. Margot caught just enough of a glimpse to see a male driver and a female passenger.

Margot straightened, wincing in discomfort as Sam marched out the front door leading Rider Arthur handcuffed ahead of her. He was limping as she led him to the other squad car. Margot spotted blood on his pantleg realizing Sam had wounded him.

That meant Trent was the one who'd

been driving the other truck with his wife in the passenger seat.

Margot's stomach sank as she realized their likely destination.

The other two officers darted out from behind the cover of their doors as more sirens wailed in the distance, signaling reinforcements. Margot eased herself out of the passenger seat and staggered towards her cousin.

"Trent and his wife got away," she said.

Sam shoved Rider at onc of the other officers. "You're sure?"

"Yes. I think they might be going to the hospital. What if they're going to finish what they started?" Margot's mouth went dry by the end of her statement.

10

Before Margot knew what was happening, police swarmed the property. Two pairs of uniformed officers approached the house from opposite directions. She could hear them calling "clear" as they moved through the house.

"You're sure there's a kid in there?" one of them asked of Sam as they reappeared empty-handed.

Sam eyed Margot. "You're absolutely certain of what you saw?"

"Absolutely. Did you check the basement?'

"We didn't find a basement," the officer answered.

Anger darkened Sam's usually pale features as she marched to where Rider was being treated by paramedics for his leg wound.

"Tell me where that little girl is hiding," Sam demanded.

Rider looked like he wasn't going to respond until his lower lip shook and tears began to well up in his eyes. "This was all Trent."

"That doesn't answer my question," Sam replied, stepping closer.

"There's a hidden panel behind the stairs. She might be there."

Sam turned to Margot. "Come on."

They headed inside and Margot couldn't help shivering at stepping into the place that Olivia had called her prison for so long. She spotted children's toys strewn in the living room: partially-dressed dolls, blocks, and paper and crayons.

They approached the staircase and at first glance, there appeared to be nothing unusual about it. Margot moved forward and ran her fingers along the wood paneling of the wall until she found a notch that didn't seem to be part of the actual design.

"I think I found it," she said and gave it a push.

The panel clicked and swung inward, revealing a set of dimly lit stairs descending into the darkness. Sam stepped in front of Margot and led the way down. The stairs whined loudly under their weight. If anyone was in fact down there, Sam and Margot's arrival would not be a surprise.

Sam stopped at the bottom of the stairs, groping along the wall until she found a light switch. She flipped it on to find a bed shoved in one corner. There were no windows. A rudimentary toilet and sewage system took up much of the rest of the space.

A little girl lay curled up on the bed, a teddy bear clutched to her chest. She looked a lot like Olivia and Penelope with fair skin and bright green eyes. Her hair was a few shades lighter, but Margot suspected that came from the girl's father. Her whole frame shook as they approached. Sam, who'd been holding her weapon at her side, holstered it and slowly approached, hands held up in front of her.

"Hi, there. What's your name?" Sam said in a soft tone.

The girl curled closer to the wall and buried her face in the pillow. Margot stepped past her cousin and crouched down in front of the girl, doing her best to hide her pain that the simple movement caused.

"I know you're scared. You want your mom, don't you, sweetie," Margot whispered.

"She went away," the girl mumbled into the bear's soft fur.

"Can you tell us your name?"

"Penny."

Breath caught in Margot's throat. Of course, that was her name. How could Olivia not have wanted to find a way to honor her sister, even if Penelope's end had been stained with tragedy. Even if Olivia felt guilt for not stopping Penelope from taking her own life.

"My name is Margot and this is Sam. She's a police officer. Do you know what a police officer is?"

Penny nodded. "Mama says they help people."

"That's right. We can take you to see your mama," Margot said and extended her hand.

Penny shook her head. "Mama D said my mama went away and isn't coming back."

Margot sighed. "Well, I know for a fact that isn't true. I saw your Mama earlier and she's very worried about you. I think it would make her really happy to see you."

Penny considered Margot's words for a long moment before uncurling from her position. She kept one arm tightened protectively around her bear as Sam led the way back up to the first floor and out into the afternoon light. She was beginning to regret forgoing that dose of pain medication as the aches in her body intensified yet again. Still, she had more pressing concerns. She needed to reunite this child with her mother. And perhaps more importantly, they needed to stop Trent and Darlene from hurting Olivia any more.

"There's a hidden basement room behind the stairs. Get techs down there to process it," Sam said to the closest officer. The ambulance with Rider in it had already left. Penny clung tight to Margot's hand, her eyes going wide at the number of people entering her house.

"We should get another ambulance here. Let the paramedics check her out," Margot suggested to Sam.

"I know. But we can't just leave her. And if you're right about Trent and Darlene and where they're heading …"

"You should do this by the book," Margot said, even though she wanted to climb into the squad car with her and speed off to the hospital.

"This is Officer Raymond," Sam said into her radio. "I'm going to need another ambulance sent to the Arthur property. I also need confirmation on the units that were sent to the hospital."

A voice on the radio responded, "Another ambulance is on its way. One unit arrived at the hospital."

"Send everyone you've got," Sam said. "We have two perps on their way now and we think they may be going after the Jane Doe."

"All available units, proceed to the hospital," the dispatcher confirmed.

"I'll wait with her," Margot said, hoping Sam would take the hint and make the daring rescue.

"Are you sure?" Sam's forehead wrinkled in concern.

"Please go. Protect Olivia."

Sam jogged around the hood of her squad car. Wanda remained in the backseat, looking shell-shocked about everything going on around her. Margot pulled Penny close as more cars peeled out of the yard following after Sam.

"Penny, honey, can I ask you some questions while we wait for the ambulance?" Margot asked.

"Okay."

"Can you tell me who your daddy is? Do you know his name?"

Penny wrinkled her nose, let go of Margot's hand and her fingers moved as if she were practicing her letters. "Rider," she finally answered.

"That's really good. And you live with your Daddy and Mama?"

"And Mama D and Daddy T."

"Oh?" The poor child had to be so confused.

Penny nodded her head, her chin bobbing up and down. "They say I have to tell everyone they are my mama and daddy when we go outside. But we don't go outside a lot."

"Were you hiding in the basement from all the loud noises?"

Penny shook her head. "I missed Mama. She said she was going to come back and get me. But she didn't."

"She got hurt when she was leaving. But I know she wants you to be safe. Does your mama stay down there all the time?"

"Yes."

"What about you? Do you have your own room?"

"I like to stay with Mama but it makes Mama D mad. She says that she is supposed to be my mama."

Margot now wondered whether it had been Trent that had chased after Margot the day before or if Darlene had been the one behind the wheel.

The ambulance appeared, sirens blaring and lights flashing. Penny latched onto Margot's hand again.

"It's okay. These nice people are going to look at you to make sure you aren't hurt."

"I want to see Mama."

"They're going to take us to where she is. I promise. You're being so brave."

The lead paramedic climbed out of the passenger side of the ambulance and opened the back up. She approached slowly.

"Hi there, sweetie. Can you do me a favor

and climb up here so we can take a look at you? Your bear can come with you."

Penny squeezed Margot's hand. "Can she come, too?"

"Of course."

Penny let go of Margot's hand long enough to crawl up into the ambulance and settle onto the gurney. Margot climbed in behind them and sat beside the child.

"Penny, did your mama leave the house a lot?"

"No. Daddy always keeps the secret door closed."

"So, do you know how she got out?"

"I saw Mama D open it. Then I went down to see mama. I told her it was open and she said we had to run away, but she didn't take me with her."

Margot made a mental note of everything Penny had told her. She had no doubt that Sam would need to interview the little girl. It would be useful to make sure her story didn't change once she was in the presence of the adults in her life.

The paramedic fastened a blood pressure cuff around Penny's small arm and put a thermometer under her tongue. The rig's engine revved to life and the wheels trundled over the gravel driveway back to the road.

"I was one of the medics that brought you in earlier," the medic said, eyeing Margot.

"Mostly bumps and bruises," Margot said, trying to brush off her own pain.

"You're brave going out after that accident."

".I couldn't say no. A friend needed my help"

"I know you served before you became the minister. I didn't realize you were so ..." the paramedic trailed off, eyeing Penny.

"I believe that whatever has been put in my path is for a reason. Sometimes God wants me to use my skills in other ways."

The ambulance stopped and the medic

moved to open the door. A pair of police officers waited to escort them inside. Margot scanned the faces of the nurses and doctors, hoping to find a familiar face. She needed to know if Olivia was okay. Had Sam gotten to her in time? Did she stop whatever Trent and Darlene had planned?

"Penny, this officer is going to stay with you," Margot said. "I'll be right back. I'm going to find your Mama."

"Promise?" Penny whispered.

Margot squeezed the girl's hand tight. "I promise."

She took off through the maze of hallways from the emergency room to the back of the hospital where Olivia had been placed. As she drew closer, she could hear raised voices. One of them belonged to her cousin.

"I'm going to tell you one more time, put the gun down and step away from the bed."

Margot's heart pounded in her chest as she moved closer until she could just barely peer into the room. Sam stood with her back to the hallway, blocking the only way in or out of the room. Olivia lay in bed with a gun pressed to her temple. Not by Trent, but by Darlene.

As Margot now surmised, Darlene wanted Penny's real mother out of the picture. She was willing to go to whatever lengths it took, even murder. Too bad the little girl was firmly attached to Olivia.

"Stay out of this," Darlene snapped.

Trent stood by her side, looking unsurprised by the entire turn of events. He made no move to stop his wife. If Olivia's tale was true, he'd orchestrated the plan to hide Penelope's body and imprison Olivia. Had he convinced Darlene to do the dirty work for him now?

"Darlene, look at me," Sam said.

"I said stay out of this," she shouted.

"I think we all know I can't do that. I want to hear what's going on from you. Can you at least tell me that much, so I understand how we got here?"

"She wants to take my baby away from me!"

"She's not yours," Olivia sobbed, thick teardrops sliding down her cheeks and dripping onto the blanket beneath her. Her right hand was concealed under the blanket.

If Margot had to guess, Olivia was holding tight to Margot's dog tags and cross.

Margot wanted to help, but getting into the room and interrupting Sam's negotiating would be a bad idea. Besides, Darlene didn't need another target.

"Penny is your daughter?" Sam said, acting as if Olivia hadn't spoken.

"Of course, she is." Darlene looked to her husband. "You said she's mine. You promised."

Trent remained silent, stoic. Sam used the momentary distraction to take another step into the room and move closer to Olivia.

"Darlene, did you shoot Olivia?" Sam probed.

"It wasn't supposed to work out like this. And then that priest got involved. We had to get her out of the way."

Margot watched as Sam bristled, her shoulder muscles tightening. She clearly didn't like the insinuation that Darlene and Trent had intended far worse consequences for Margot than a possible concussion and fractured ribs. Margot didn't disagree. In fact, the realization that they'd intended to kill her sent chills down her spine.

"You did *what* to Margot?" Olivia demanded, her tone growing stronger. She sat up, causing the gun to move even closer to her temple.

"Olivia, Margot is fine," Sam said, trying to regain control of the conversation. "Look, Darlene, we already know that your husband paid off Wanda Lawrence to lie to the police years ago about Penelope and Olivia's disappearance. He's going away for a long time. And, based on what you're saying right now, it sounds like you might be joining him, too. Unless you help me out here."

"Wanda didn't do anything she didn't want to do," Trent scoffed, finally joining the conversation.

"So, you're admitting you paid her to lie?" Sam prompted.

Trent shrugged. "I did what I had to do. Just like my Darlene, here."

"Your brother is already cooperating with us. So, whatever you think you're going to get out of this, I can assure you it won't happen," Sam replied.

Margot had no way of knowing if that was true. Given Rider's expression of remorse after being arrested, it was definitely a possibility. Yes, he'd been horrible to Penelope, but perhaps his behavior had been more influenced by his older brother than any of them had realized.

"Darlene, I don't want to have to shoot you," Sam said. "And I'm sure you think that you can pull the trigger faster than me, but you're wrong. I won't miss either."

Olivia didn't give Darlene time to respond to Sam's words. She pulled her uninjured arm from beneath the blankets and slammed her fist—wrapped in the chain and cross— into Darlene's jaw.

The unexpected blow sent the woman staggering backward and in her haste to assess her injured face, she let the gun slip from her fingers.

Trent moved for the gun, but Sam moved faster than any human should be able to and scooped up the gun before Trent could lay a finger on it.

Margot then stepped into the room. She grabbed a handful of tissues sitting on a nearby tray and held out her hand to Sam.

Sam deposited the gun carefully, making sure that Margot didn't contaminate it with her prints.

Margot darted from the room and passed it off to one of the officers who had come looking for them.

When Margot returned to the room, Darlene was already in handcuffs and Trent had his hands raised. It was not the outcome they'd been expecting, but it was the right one. Olivia and Penny could be reunited. Now Olivia could live her own life free from the horrors that had been inflicted upon her. And the Arthurs would serve justice.

Margot waited while the officers escorted Darlene and Trent from the room before going in. Olivia, now out of adrenaline slumped against the pillows. The single blow had worn her out. She held her hand out, shaking the chain from around her fingers.

"You were right, this did come in handy," Olivia said with a weak smile.

Margot took the tags and cross back from her slipping them over her head. "You're going to get tired of hearing this, but I need to say it. I am so sorry for everything you've gone through. I'm a pretty good listener if you need someone to talk to. It doesn't have to be now or even soon, but when you're ready, I'll be here."

"Thank you."

"Penny is getting checked out by doctors right now. If you want, I can let them know you're ready to see her. I know she's going to be happy to see you."

"I'm sorry I didn't tell you about her from the beginning. I was just so scared that they would hurt her."

Margot patted Olivia's hand. "You were protecting your daughter."

"She couldn't have children … Darlene, I mean. They tried for a while before the doctor said she wasn't able to get pregnant."

"So, they decided to make you carry a child."

"She knew one of the midwives here who made house calls. They paid her to keep quiet." Margot knew Sam would make sure the midwife was held accountable for her role in all of this.

"Oh my, that explains why you were so jumpy about the doctor earlier."

"Yes."

"Is Rider the father?"

"Reluctantly."

"He raped you?"

"Uh, yes … He didn't want to do it, either."

"It was all really Trent's idea, wasn't it? Hiding Penelope's remains, keeping you locked up?"

"Yes. Rider went along with it because he was grieving over losing Penelope. But as time went by, he came to accept the idea that just because Penelope and I were twins didn't really mean we were the same. I was never going to love him, no matter how much Trent tried to push him. Trent threatened to pin everything on Rider if he didn't father a child with me."

Margot wanted to take Olivia at her word, but the way she spoke about Rider reminded her of Stockholm syndrome. She had read accounts of victims released from prolonged captivity, who had suffered the same. It was much like what Dustin Grady had succumbed to from Conrad Baptiste's delusions over the years.

"He still participated in keeping you captive, even if he wasn't a willing participant in the end. You know that, right?"

"I know. I'm not saying I forgive him for what he did to me and my sister. I want him to face justice for the things he did. I also know he idolized his brother. So much of what he did was because Trent goaded him into it. The drinking, the abuse, all came from wanting to prove himself to his brother. Their sibling bond is stronger than a lot of people realize."

"We're going to make sure they are held accountable for everything."

Their conversation was cut short by a child's chattering coming from the hallway. Penny stuck her head around the corner and peered into the room. Immediately, the little girl's face brightened and Olivia's did, too.

"Baby," she cooed.

"Mama! Margot said you wanted to come back and get me but you got hurt," Penny said as she raced to her mother's bedside.

"I would never leave you, sweetheart."

Margot knew Olivia now faced a difficult situation. How did she explain to a child that her father, aunt, and uncle—whom she viewed as pseudo parents—were going to prison for a very long time? How long would it take for them to find a new normal?

11

<hr>

Reverend Hawley had been kind enough to step up and lead services while Margot recuperated. All of the exertion in rescuing Penny and reuniting her with her mother Olivia, had taken a toll on Margot's body. In truth, one that she hadn't expected. She was sitting on her couch and enjoying a glass of fresh-squeezed lemonade when her cell phone buzzed with an incoming text message.

It was from Sam, letting Margot know she'd arrived with dinner.

"The door is open," Margot called. It had been over a week since her accident. She was just now getting comfortable with not bolting the door the moment she entered the apartment.

The front door opened and closed. Margot listened to her cousin moving around in the kitchen. The crinkle of a delivery bag betrayed their meal before the smell of Chinese food wafted through the apartment.

"How are you feeling?" Sam asked and strode into the living room wearing a tank top and shorts. She was definitely off duty.

"Better. I should be good to go back to work tomorrow. Just in time to welcome Olivia and Penny back into the community."

"How has their transition been?" Sam set take out containers on the table in front of the couch.

"Rough. Olivia told me that Penny cried the first few nights they were in the hotel after they got out of the hospital. But Olivia's parents were thrilled to have her back."

Sam retreated into the kitchen to grab plates and utensils. From the other room, she called, "How did they take the news that their other daughter had been dead all this time?"

"It was hard for them. I know Olivia tries to hide it, but I think she's suffering from survivor's guilt." Margot understood that feeling too well herself. "Thankfully I don't think her parents blame her for what happened."

Setting plates down, Sam settled on the couch beside Margot. "I honestly couldn't imagine dealing with everything she went through and still be able to see the good in people. Not to mention experience the joy of her own little girl."

"She was always a strong person. She didn't let her ordeal beat her down," Margot answered and scooped fried rice from one of the containers onto a plate.

"I'm still trying to wrap my head around the fact she was literally in town this whole time and no one noticed anything … for twenty years."

"When you had people willing to cover things up for money, sadly it isn't that hard to believe," Margot commented, disappointment coloring her tone.

"That's another thing. How could all of those people do that? They had to know something bad was going on."

"Everybody sins. It's part of the human condition. But in the end, enough people came forward and admitted what they had done, and you were able to stop two people from committing horrible crimes. And everyone involved will face the consequences of their actions."

Sam arched an eyebrow. "You're telling me you weren't judging these people for their actions? Even you aren't a saint."

"I'm not perfect, no. And I'll admit I did judge them, especially Wanda. I thought I knew her and her character. It turned out I was wrong. But I'm glad we were able to reunite Olivia and Penny, a happy ending after everything."

"Rider gave a full confession, too. He implicated Trent and Darlene for their parts in what had happened. He even showed us where they'd buried Penelope's body. The tests haven't come back yet, but I can't imagine they would have a random woman's body buried in their backyard."

"He cut a deal?'

"It's not that unheard of for co-conspirators to turn on each other for the possibility of less jail time. He's agreed to testify against his brother."

"After all the loyalty he paid Trent over the years?" Margot said in surprise.

Sam nodded. "I wasn't expecting it, either. I guess under all of his bravado, he still had a conscience." After a moment of silence, Sam said, "I guess Olivia was right and he got fed up with what Trent was having him to do."

Repentance could be a strong motivator. If Rider did believe in God or any higher being, absolving himself of his crimes—or at least admitting to his sins—was a step in the right direction. He might see his child before she turned eighteen. Although Margot doubted Olivia would be comfortable allowing her daughter to know the man who'd forced her to bear his child.

"It has been one heck of a year since you got back, hasn't it?" Sam said and piled Kung Pao Chicken onto her plate.

Margot took the container from Sam, considering her cousin's words. Much of the year had been painful and filled with heartache. But it also provided the town a chance to heal some old wounds. Not only that, Margot had been able to put some of her own ghosts to rest.

"Yes, it has. But it hasn't been all bad. You and I reconnected, I found my next calling on my journey of faith, we saved some lives, and reunited families who thought they would be forever broken. Not bad for a police officer and a minister."

"Who would have thought all those years ago when we were little girls, we'd end up sitting here having solved three murders and given an entire town closure," Sam marveled.

"We make a good team," Margot agreed.

"I mean, it wasn't always by the book, but I don't think I could have done it without you."

"You are more than capable, Sam. Don't sell yourself short."

"But you see things in a different way, with a certain perspective. I wouldn't have come up with that on my own. Or if I had, I wouldn't have been fast enough. You have a way with people. You get them to trust you and open up to you in a way I can't."

"Then there was clearly a reason it was you who answered that 9-1-1 call when Warren Nesbit died," Margot said. "We were both put on this path for a reason. We've both grown as people and together as family."

Margot held up her glass and waited for Sam to do the same.

"To us," Margot said.

They clinked glasses.

Sam added, "Just promise me, we won't be solving any murders for at least a little while."

"It's a deal." Besides, Margot couldn't believe the town had any more secrets left to unearth. What they had endured over the last nine months was more than enough to last them a lifetime.

Joan Margot in hunting down the culprit in three more faith-filled mysteries. Download Reverend Margot Quade Cozy Mysteries Volume 2 to solve the case today.

Join Sarah's newsletter for the latest updates! Subscribe

ABOUT THE AUTHOR

S.E. Biglow is the pen name of *USA Today* bestselling author Sarah Biglow. She lives in Massachusetts with her husband and son. She is a licensed attorney and spends her days combatting employment discrimination as an Investigator with the Massachusetts Commission Against Discrimination.

You can find an up-to-date list of all my books here